A Note from the Author

First off—thank you!. Whether you picked this up out of curiosity, boredom, or because someone guilt-tripped you into it… you're here, and that means the world.

Heidi Evervale began life as a happy accident—a simple misfire in perspective on a splash page I drew of Batgirl. That accident lit a spark I didn't expect, and it's one that's driven me to work on some part of this world nearly every day since.

Originally, this whole thing was called Zombie Ninja Rock Vampire (some of you may remember that chaotic little title). It was meant to be a goofy comic strip—think Garfield meets Buffy, only with more eyeliner and fewer lasagnas. Heidi was supposed to be a one-panel gag character: her mum a vampire, her dad a zombie, and her life full of weird undead mishaps. That was the plan. But apparently, my brain doesn't do simple (I know some of you will be happy to argue that point).

Instead, Heidi's backstory kept growing. And growing. Until eventually, I realised I wasn't writing jokes anymore—I was building a whole universe. I thought a comic series might do the trick… until I discovered that writing, drawing, inking, and lettering a 23-page comic every six months was like trying to shovel snow during an avalanche.

So, I switched to prose. Only took 25 years, but I was finally putting my English degree to use. Miracles do happen.

That decision cracked everything wide open. Writing the novel gave me the freedom to explore Heidi's world properly—to dive into the lore, the history, the politics, and the characters who'd been waiting patiently in the wings. It's been a wild, stubborn, oddly emotional process—but it's also been the most creatively fulfilling thing I've ever done. And hey, it's the reason you're reading this now, so I must've done something right.

As you read, you'll notice something in the top-right corner of each chapter: a suggested song. You don't need it to enjoy Heidi – Echoes of Ash: Part One — but music is a huge part of Heidi's world, and a huge part of why I wrote this the way I did. If nothing else, it's a chance to step a little deeper into her world — and come along for the ride.

And here's the cool part: you're one of the first people to read it. This isn't a wide release or some polished mass-market drop. This is the very start—the first peek into something much bigger. You're part of the small group stepping into this world before anyone else, and I honestly can't thank you enough for that. Early readers like you matter more than you know.

This is just the beginning. Heidi's story is only a small corner of the world she lives in, and trust me, it gets much,

much bigger. By the end of Part One, you'll see the cracks starting to spread—and things are only going to get louder from here.

So again—thank you. Whether this is your first step into Heidi's world or you've been following her since the zombie ninja days, I'm really glad you're here.

Now... you ready to meet Heidi?

– Wes

Heidi Evervale
Echoes of Ash

Written, drawn & created by

Wes Lawson Bowie

Echoes of Ash: Part One

© 2025 Wes Lawson Bowie

All rights reserved.

No part of this publication may be reproduced, stored in a retrieval system, or transmitted in any form or by any means—electronic, mechanical, photocopying, recording, or otherwise—without the prior written permission of the author, except for brief quotations used in critical reviews or scholarly works.

This is a work of fiction. Names, characters, places, and events are either products of the author's imagination or used fictitiously. Any resemblance to actual persons, living or dead, or actual events is purely coincidental.

First edition.

Cover and interior design by Wes Lawson Bowie.

For more information, visit:

www.BeforeHeidi.com

CONTENTS

Prologue 9

Chapter One – The Bar 19

Chapter Two – Pazuzu Town Hall 39

Chapter Three – Fallout 55

Chapter Four – Pop-Pop 81

Chapter Five – A Knock at the Gates 109

Epilogue – 猫の三姉妹 137

APPENDIX 1
Excerpts from History:
The World of Echoes of Ash 155

APPENDIX 2
A Closer Look at the NetherKind Species 209

PROLOGUE

Ellis eased the car into a shallow layby, headlights sweeping across the jagged rock face ahead. The pull-in was barely wide enough to feel safe—just a scar in the landscape carved by time and erosion. On Snake Pass, this was as close as you got to mercy. The road itself offered none. It twisted with the land—tight, narrow, and coiled like wire pulled too far.

Rain pummelled the roof in relentless sheets, each drop sharp and cold as splinters. Wind pressed hard against the chassis, rattling the frame as lorries roared past, their wake slamming into the car like waves against a lifeboat.

Ellis leaned forward, forehead resting against the steering wheel. His hands still hovered loosely around it—

gripped, not by caution, but by momentum. Like the drive hadn't quite let go of him yet.

Just a moment. A breath. A pocket of stillness on a road that rarely allowed one.

In the passenger seat, nestled in a faded baby carrier and swaddled in his old Tool hoodie, the baby stirred. One small foot wriggled free, pale toes curling as it dangled over the edge of the makeshift cocoon he'd built around her. The hoodie swallowed her whole—black, oversized, frayed at the sleeves—but it was warm, and it smelled like him. That seemed to help.

A week ago, the boot of the car had held his drum kit—kick, snare, cymbals, all crammed in with the kind of care only musicians understand. Now, it was stuffed with nappies, bottles, wipes, and a half-read manual on sleep routines. He didn't understand any of it. But he'd packed it like he was loading gear for a tour. Because that's what this was now. A different kind of tour. A different kind of noise.

Heidi made a soft, searching cry. Not distressed—just uncertain. Like she wasn't quite sure if this was the right world.

"I'm here," Ellis murmured, reaching over.

He took her hand between his thumb and finger—delicate, precise, like the whole world might shift if he let go. Her fingers closed around his instinctively. Not strong enough to hold on. Just enough to say: I'm here too.

He hadn't been asked to take her. Nina hadn't begged or pleaded. She'd just told him.

"You're the one who keeps her safe," Nina had said—Ellis's sister—between contractions, her voice calm. Certain. Like she knew something he didn't.

None of them knew Heidi would be born half vampire. Not the doctors. Not Ellis. Maybe Nina had suspected—but if she did, she took the truth with her.

Because by the time Heidi took her first breath, Nina was gone.

What followed was chaos. More doctors. More tests. Questions without answers. Panic in the corridors.

The media descended. Politicians debated. Protesters gathered. Scientists offered theories. Everyone had an opinion. But no one had a clue.

Ellis barely had time to grieve and now he had Heidi. This fragile, strange little being. Half vampire. Half human. Entirely his responsibility.

Maybe that's what Nina had meant. What she'd known.

And yet, there was one moment Ellis couldn't shake. One he'd never spoken of.

It had happened the night Heidi was born. Nina's room looked out over the rear service yard of the hospital—just bins and a loading bay. No foot traffic. No reason for anyone to be out there at night.

But as Ellis stood at the window, staring into the dark, he saw something.

A figure.

Tall. Still. Just beyond the reach of the floodlight.

There was a faint glow around it—nothing dramatic, just the sense of something lit from within, like the shimmer of heat rising off concrete. It didn't move. Didn't shift or turn. But Ellis felt it.

It was looking at him. He knew it.

He let the curtain fall.

Never told Nina. She didn't need more to carry.

By morning, Heidi was there.

And Nina was gone.

The figure? Whether it had ever really been there… Ellis never found out.

Days later, leaving the hospital with Heidi, the press had swarmed the car park. Cameras. Flashbulbs. Microphones in faces.

It wasn't defiance. It was instinct.

Some wanted to study her. Others wanted to protect her. A few wanted her erased entirely.

But to Ellis, she was just a baby. His niece. Strapped into the passenger seat, bundled in his old hoodie and a world already trying to define her.

He glanced over at her. She wasn't asleep.

Her lips were latched around his finger, suckling softly. Eyes half-closed, dazed with contentment. Three of his fingers were bound in plasters, healing from where she had previously fed. Tiny, neat punctures marked his skin. He'd found that rotating his fingers, one at a time, gave the others time to recover and Heidi was never aggressive causing pain, never frantic. It was just a need. She drank from him because it worked. Because it kept her calm. Because it stopped the crying that seemed to come from somewhere deeper than hunger.

The pink hue in her irises had deepened over the past few days—faint at first, now brighter, like the colour had been waiting to emerge.

Ellis stared for a moment, wondering how much more would change.

No one really knew what she was. And Ellis hadn't let them try to figure it out. Not yet anyway.

No tests. No sunlight. No guesses. For now.

She was his to protect.

Even if the rest of the world wanted to dissect her.

Even if he had no idea what she might become.

There'd been one decision to make, and he'd made it the moment they left the hospital—Pazuzu City.

A place built on refuge. A city carved into the Pennines where NetherKind and humans once stood side by side. A city that had made him feel welcome when the rest of the world just saw him as a drummer.

Not all NetherKind cities were like that. Some were strict, closed-off. But Pazuzu was different. Loud. Gritty. Open. If there was any place in the world that might give Heidi a chance, it was Pazuzu.

The journey still had thirty or forty minutes to go and it was past midnight. Rain was still falling.

Ellis leaned back in the driver's seat, eyes on the road ahead, then on the baby beside him.

His old life was over. And he was okay with that.

Because whatever this new life turned out to be—it was going to be one hell of a ride.

PART ONE

BLOOD & VINYL

"Let there be no doubt, this new world order possesses the promise of immense benefit, yet it also bears the grave potential to lead us to complete ruin."

- Thomas Jefferson, 1802 AD

Fugazi - Give Me The Cure

CHAPTER ONE

The Bar

Heidi couldn't recall how many drinks she'd had—and it didn't matter. The alcohol was doing its job, numbing everything while her body quietly repaired itself—cuts, bruises, and the deeper wounds she hadn't even noticed yet. Best to sit. Wait. Let it happen. There was nowhere urgent she needed to be, and the last few hours had been rough. It showed.

Grabbing at the tattered sleeve of her shirt, she tried to hook it back over her shoulder—only for it to slide off again almost instantly. It was beyond saving. A loss she actually mourned, because it wasn't just any shirt. It was her favourite band tee—an old, distressed A Perfect Circle print, worn thin with age and now bloodstained beyond redemption. The damage to her, she could live with. But this? This just pissed her off.

She turned her eyes to the rest of the bar. It had filled out a lot more while she wasn't paying attention. No familiar faces, but still a crowd she recognised. Mostly. Students, artists, lost souls.

Near the front, seated just left of the stage, two Nyssari shared a table. Their skin—one moss-dark, the other olive-toned—seemed to drink in the low light, softening them into the shadows. Neither spoke. They didn't need to. Nyssari rarely filled silence with noise. Instead, their eyes tracked the bar, the crowd, the subtle movements of people shifting drinks, checking phones, enjoying each other's company. It wasn't scrutiny—it was presence. Still, aware, like they were listening to something unspoken in the room's rhythm.

They weren't here for her, Heidi was sure of that. They were just… here. Like everyone else. A drink, a show, maybe the need for company without the burden of conversation.

She respected that.

One of them, the darker of the two, tapped their finger against the condensation on their glass in a slow, steady rhythm. The other followed suit a moment later—not mimicry, not a signal, just a quiet echo. A flow. Heidi remembered Mijo once calling it 'Tuning'. Aligning with the space around you. It was something Nyssari did when they were somewhere they felt safe.

Over at the far end of the bar, down from where Heidi sat, two Vaylen sat in quiet conversation, eyes never leaving each other. Their hands stayed still, but the soft flicker of their bioluminescent markings told another story. Colours pulsed across their forearms through their veins in geometric waves—strands of cool blue shifting to dark, then a sudden spark of white. A joke, maybe. One of them smirked. The other's markings stuttered like static—amusement, or maybe a playful insult.

Vaylens called it Luma. Their own silent language. No one outside their species could speak it, and most couldn't read it either. Heidi only knew a few fragments—mostly from Connor. Enough to spot a greeting. A warning. A name. But this wasn't that. This was pure Luma flowing.

It was beautiful in a way she couldn't explain.

And yet, it made her feel even further away from everything.

Vaylen with glowing veins. Nyssari with skin like moss. Julpa towering over everyone, all tusks and quiet strength.

And then there was her.

Skin pale enough to look grey beneath streetlights. Eyes tinted faintly pink—a diluted trace of vampire red, the doctors had said, back when they still poked and prodded, trying to categorise her.

As if a diagnosis might make her easier to explain.

Then there was the hair. Black and white streaks that refused to be tamed. Not dyed, not styled—just there, loud and strange, falling past her shoulders when she let it.

She wasn't one thing or the other. No legacy to fall back on. No tribe. No rulebook.

Just fragments of something older than memory—tied to a bloodline that had long since vanished behind closed doors and shadowed borders.

She wasn't lost—just finding her own way.

Dropping her gaze, she let the rim of the glass rest against her lips and unlocked her phone again—out of habit more than the need. Notifications flooded in. Ellis. Abi. Connor. All asking the same thing: Are you okay? Where are you? Blah blah blah.

No. She wasn't okay. Far from it. Replying now was pointless and she cycled through them locating the live news feeds and updates.

The headlines hadn't changed. Chaos. Disruption. Infrastructure on the brink. Three dots danced and a new headline appeared, colder than the rest:

Heidi Evervale at Heart of Destruction.

Her stomach knotted. There it was. She didn't need to read the attached articles, she'd witnessed it all firsthand. Heidi's curiosity was how it was being reported—how the city, and in turn the world, would see it. Not the truth of the event, but how it had been interpreted. All it would take was one headline with her name front and centre, and here it was.

Once again, thrust into the spotlight for all the wrong reasons. The last time, she had no control over it, she'd only just been born, and the world was reacting to uncertainty. How was she possible? Will there be more? She's a vampire and a human—how? Questions that were still unanswered.

At age twenty-three, she was now accountable for her actions. This time, Heidi thought, the world wouldn't so easily forget. And she doubted it would forgive at all.

Every blow she'd taken today felt pointless, Evelyn had walked away, untouched. Had Evelyn set her up to fail? The question burned through her mind mirroring the sting of the whisky hitting the back of her throat. Evelyn had won, the world was about to change forever, and Heidi couldn't shake the feeling that it was all her fault.

Better have another drink then she thought.

She took a sip of whisky, the metallic tang of blood no longer blending with it. The rim of the glass smudged—dried blood from where her lip had been split open. Hit hard. Repeatedly. Enough to rattle her teeth. Enough to lose a few.

Being half-human meant she felt everything. Every cracked bone, every tear of muscle. Pain didn't linger long—but she felt it all.

The cuts and bruises she'd walked in with, including the deep gash in her side, had already faded to pale traces. Ghosts on her skin. But the ache was still there, sitting beneath the surface like a reminder. A warning. She wasn't invincible.

The Rabbit Hole was James' bar. He was one of the first to help Ellis and Mijo in the early days when they were establishing their own live music venue, The Pit, which Heidi also called home. The flat with Ellis was just somewhere she slept.

James, a human like Ellis, had thankfully been on duty when she stumbled in—bloodied and barely standing. He knew better than to ask what she was running from.

Other bar staff had clocked on at The Rabbit Hole since Heidi's first drink, most arriving late thanks to the city-wide traffic chaos—another ripple from her. If anyone else other than James had been behind the bar, they would've refused to serve her. Maybe even kick her out.

James hadn't asked questions. She hadn't offered answers. Her black-and-white hair hung like a curtain, hiding bruises as she drained one glass after another. No one had noticed her yet. But it wouldn't be long. And she wasn't ready to be found.

She reached for James' hoodie—the one he'd offered when she first arrived. A subtle hint that she looked like shit. If you didn't know who Heidi Evervale was before today, you sure as hell did now. Having a contingent of foreign soldiers camped outside your city for the past few days tended to make international news. Especially when you were the reason they were there.

She slid her arms into the hoodie, wincing at the motion, and pulled it over her shoulders, hood lifted over her head. It was two sizes too big. Perfect. She could see out. No one could see in.

Through the speakers, Joe Lally's deep bassline muffled the murmur of the crowd in The Rabbit Hole. James had given her control of the jukebox—his one regret as now they were stuck with '90s melancholy with a sprinkle of 80s.

As he had done since her arrival, James reached for the bottle and refilled her empty glass, understanding she wasn't leaving anytime soon. He broke the silence, his voice gentle, knowing when someone wanted to be left alone.

"Ow you feelin'?"

Heidi smirked. "Like I look."

"Tha' bad, huh? Owt I can do?

"Leave the bottle?"

"Don' be obvious with it." He placed the bottle behind the bar within Heidi's reach but out of sight of everyone else. He'd known Heidi since she was a toddler and now considered her to be a friend. She downed her drink and immediately reached for the bottle to pour another as James was thumb tapping out a message on his phone.

Without waiting for a reply, he locked the screen and placed it face down on the bar just as a customer approached.

"Hey, mind if there's a change in the music? Something more upbeat?" the guy asked, nodding toward the jukebox.

James gave a subtle tilt of his head to where Heidi was perched on her stool. "She's got the reins tonight," he said, voice low.

The guy followed his gaze. Heidi sat, cloaked, face hidden beneath the shadow of the hood, a fresh drink in her hand. She didn't move. She didn't need to.

"Right," the guy murmured, backing off to where he came from.

"When does the gig start?" Heidi asked glaring into her glass, unaware her music taste had just been indirectly questioned.

"Bout seven-thirty. Faceless Man round eight-thirty."

"Good. I need to hear some sad songs to make me feel better."

She wiped her lips and corners of her mouth with her arm, removing the dry crusts of blood that had built up. Her teeth had returned, one by one—regrown clean, white, sharp. Including the fang that was pretty much a key part of her signature look, not that she was trying.

Probing it gently with her tongue, she found herself reflecting on the time she used to pull them out—every morning before school, hoping it might help her blend in. Be accepted. Feel normal.

It wasn't just the fangs. It was being different in a city full of different.

Back then, she'd stand at the mirror before school, pliers in hand, trembling. Staring at her reflection. Summoning the courage, tears threatening, and with a swift motion—clamp, yank—a fang came free. Then the other.

Ellis never knew. By the time she arrived at The Pit after finishing school, her fangs had already grown back—like they'd never left.

The routine lasted a week, maybe a little longer, before he found out.

He'd been furious—at himself. Not at her.

How could he have missed it, he asked himself. She made it clear right there and then that this wasn't about him—that his guilt, his anger at himself, his need to fix things weren't what she needed. She was the one pulling her own teeth out, not him. The one walking into school every morning with a mouth full of pain, a body trying to heal before lunch. It wasn't his shame to carry, no matter how much he wanted to. She didn't need his guilt. She needed him to see her—not his reflection in her struggle. It was one of the first times she'd stood up to him. Certainly not the last.

When Ellis saw the truth written on her face, they talked. Really talked. And for the first time, she started to believe she might be okay.

Since then, they'd been open. Honest.

Now, she bore her fangs openly. No apologies.

This girl, with blood on her mouth and whisky in hand—she'd stopped hiding a long time ago.

But Ellis… he still carried the guilt. But then what parent wouldn't. Thankfully he had The Pit as a welcome distraction when times called for it.

Ellis lived and breathed music—every chord progression, every sweat-drenched stage, every band that deserved to be heard. That passion had shaped Heidi's world, passed down like a second language. She took what he taught her and ran with it, discovering her own sounds, her own obsessions—diving deep into bands Ellis didn't even know existed. She played in a few bands herself. Got kicked out of most. Technically, she was gifted—naturally brilliant with a guitar in her hands—but she had a habit of trying to control the music. Not out of ego. Just because she knew she could do it better.

Music was the one place she never second-guessed herself. Where her instincts were sharp, her choices clear. She only wished that same certainty came with everything else in her life.

When it came to business, to logistics and licensing and keeping the lights on, Ellis fell short. Fortunately, James had never viewed him as competition. He saw a collaborator. A fellow believer in the noise, the community, the raw energy of live performance. In time, their mutual respect grew into friendship—built on late nights, loaded vans, and one shared mission: to get as many bands on stage as possible, and keep the music alive in Pazuzu City.

Tonight was no different. Heidi had purchased a ticket for the evening's gig months ago to see The Faceless Man, but today's events had led her to arrive earlier, not in the condition that she had originally planned. Initially, the bar had been a quiet refuge, with just a few others scattered about. As 6 p.m. approached, the atmosphere shifted; attendees began to fill the space, choosing seats and tables before the small stage, their drinks lined up as they chatted among themselves. A city on fire wouldn't stop these people getting to a gig—life still moved on regardless of what was happening in the world. Usually, Heidi would have joined them, potentially meeting new friends who shared her love for music. Tonight, she wasn't in the mood—and she knew her appearance would keep people away.

She closed her eyes for a moment, feeling the fang with her tongue again.

Quiet. Still. She wondered if things would ever be the same again. Somehow, she'd managed to push the world to the brink of war. Just by existing.

She shifted on the barstool, the worn leather creaking beneath her, and reached for her glass. As her fingers brushed the rim, her gaze fell to the floor beside her—and froze.

Leaning against the bar, partially obscured by the folds of James's oversized hoodie, was the sword. She vaguely remembered carrying something as she walked into The

Rabbit Hole—confused from concussion or not, she remembered one thing—it was Evelyn's sword.

Stared at it, a jolt of recognition sparking through the haze of alcohol and exhaustion. She'd walked away from the confrontation with it, but not intentionally.

The weapon rested with an unsettling stillness, its hilt wrapped in dark leather bindings that spiralled down to the crossguard. The blade, sheathed in a scabbard of worn black lacquer, bore subtle etchings that caught the dim bar light—symbols she didn't recognise. The curvature of the sheath hinted at the blade's elegant arc, a design she associated with ceremonial displays or martial arts films, not real-life encounters.

Her mind drifted back to the fight. The moment when Evelyn had lunged, sword arcing toward her. Instinct had driven Heidi to parry, her hand reaching out, fingers grazing the hilt. In that instant, a flicker of blue light had pulsed beneath the bindings of the sword hilt—a brief, ethereal glow, like a candle flame whipped by a sudden gust. It had vanished as quickly as it appeared, leaving her questioning whether she'd seen it at all.

When she came to, the sword was by her side. Evelyn nowhere to be seen. She'd picked it up carefully, gripping it by the scabbard, deliberately avoiding the hilt. Even now, she hadn't touched it directly since.

She took another sip of her drink, the whisky burning a path down her throat, and glanced around the bar. The crowd had thickened, voices rising in a low hum of anticipation for the night's performance. No one was paying attention to her. Which meant her attention was pulled towards the sword.

Heidi reached down, fingers hovering over the hilt. She hesitated, then pulled back. Not yet. She wasn't ready to confront whatever shit came with that. She'd had enough for one day.

For now, it would remain by her side, a silent companion in the dim glow of The Rabbit Hole.

Her mind drifted—to Evelyn. To her face. Her voice. Echoed too easily in Heidi's mind. Still soft. Still sure.

"We're not so different, you and I." The last thing Evelyn said to her.

Heidi slammed the thought away with another swig and whispered to herself.

"Yeah…but I've got your sword, fucker."

It felt like a small win. And she'd take that. For now.

Radiohead - There There

CHAPTER TWO

Rose

Rose leaned against the balcony rail, looking out over Pazuzu City. The sky was warm and blue. Summer in the Pennines always brought that crisp, clean air. But there, in the distance, a column of thick black smoke climbed above the sprawling city line, shrouding the flames of whatever was on fire raging beneath it. A reminder that this was far from a normal day—if such a thing even existed anymore. From this high up, it looked almost peaceful. A distant calm that didn't match the storm escalating behind her.

Inside her office, voices clashed—each one rising above the next in a desperate attempt to restore order, only adding to the chaos bleeding through their phones to others across the city doing the same. This was her city. Her responsibility. Not just to govern, but to hold together—even now, as it threatened to come apart at the seams. With British troops stationed outside all four gates, if Heidi wasn't in their custody by midnight, Pazuzu would be deemed complicit—along with the rest of the NetherKind Commonwealth. And then, War. All thanks to Heidi. It was already 6pm.

The video call with her peers an hour earlier had gone exactly as she'd expected—poorly. And with the pressure mounting, it had only confirmed what she already feared: she was on her own. Her expectations had been low, and the call didn't even try to exceed them. The other NetherKind cities from around the world—Balam, Sachamama, New Hinode—even Ch'i-Lin—had all joined. Everyone had an opinion. No one had a solution. Ch'i-Lin, naturally, said nothing. Of course they didn't. Always the observer, collecting information without ever offering any of their own. Supportive, hesitant, dismissive—the tone varied, but the undercurrent was the same: unease. Every one of them was nervous.

Everyone except Rose.

She'd been thrown into this under circumstances she didn't choose. But if she had to carry the weight, then she'd carry it her way. No compromises. No deference. This was going to go the way she decided. No one else. Not even Heidi.

Heidi—the one Rose had previously risked her career for—had now become the face of a new crisis. And Rose wasn't sure she could defend Heidi again. The one she'd fought for in court. The one she'd defended when no one else would. Rose took chances in those early days and that case changed everything. It made her who she was now: Mayor of Pazuzu City. The first human ever elected to govern a NetherKind city. Maybe this time, doing the right thing meant doing something… less than favourable.

Back then, the risk had felt worth it. Now? She wasn't so sure. If that same choice stood before her again? No. She wouldn't make it. And she wasn't too proud to admit that.

Heidi was a girl with no people. A hybrid in a city built on bloodlines. The NetherKind Cities were formed by tribes, by history, by species who knew exactly where they belonged. And then there was Heidi—one of one. No wonder the world didn't know what to do with her. No wonder the world wanted her gone—until Rose stepped in.

That was then. This was now. And now... Rose was very likely to be the last human ever elected to govern a NetherKind City.

Pazuzu was the third of the twelve NetherKind Cities to rise from the wreckage of the Ash Dawn, a catastrophic series of events at the turn of the 16th Century, led by humans that almost wiped out the NetherKind species known as Vampire. The two NetherKind cities of, Balam in the United States, and Malphas in Germany, preceded Pazuzu. All cities built from ruin, grit, and defiance. Within their walls, the five NetherKind species began to forge a new society—separate from the humans, the majority of whom could no longer be trusted. Uncertain if they would be next, the other species abandoned the settlements they had shared with humans for centuries. The Vaylen, the Julpa, the Nyssari. Together they chose unity over uncertainty. The Aetherien, already nomadic by nature, continued their solitary paths—appearing only when and where they were drawn. What was left of the Vampires vanished to their own hidden settlements, seldom making scarce appearances elsewhere and only out of necessity. Born of catastrophe, the Cities endured through will, hope, and the shared belief that survival demanded something new.

And here Rose stood, charged with holding Pazuzu together as it tilted toward collapse—as humans, once again, raised the question: could they be trusted? Rose had a choice to make. Handover Heidi, or do everything in her power to protect her. Either way, she lost. To top it off, no one had a clue where she was and the decanted whisky back in her office was starting to make the most sense.

"Where's Heidi now?!" The voice rose above the others—Adam, Rose's assistant. "You don't know?! What about Evelyn Shaw?... Are you fucking kidding me?!" Rose didn't need to hear the reply to know the answer. They didn't know where Evelyn was either. "They've turned half the city upside down and there's no trace of them? Is that what you're actually telling me?"

Adam had appeared in the doorway between the balcony and the office, one hand clamped over the mouthpiece of his phone. "Miss Calloway, they—"

Rose spun around and held out her hand. Whatever patience she'd started the morning with had long since burned off. Adam handed over the phone without hesitation or another word.

"I have a press conference in…" She checked her watch. "…precisely twenty-six minutes. That gives you twenty-five to get me answers."

She ended the call and handed the phone back to Adam.

"We don't have the luxury of asking questions that don't come with answers, Adam."

She strode from the balcony into the centre of the room, drawing eyes as she moved.

"I need everyone's attention. Now."

Conversations cut off. Heads turned. Phones lowered. Rose took her place behind her desk—not a tall woman by any stretch, but when she wanted the room, it was hers.

"This isn't something I say lightly. But right now, we've got our tail between our legs, a city held to a standstill and no fucking clue what's going on. And all I'm hearing is more questions. Here's the only one that matters: Where. Is. Heidi? That's it. Until we know, we can't move.

Then—and only then—we decide. Do we hand her over?" Rose extended her hand to the left, "Or do we close the gates?" then the right—a deliberate display, the kind taught in media training to command a room's attention. "Either way, what happens next will be out of our hands. But if we have Heidi—we have control. Without her, we might as well be piss in the wind." Rose checked her watch again. "Twenty-two minutes. Make them count."

The room exploded into motion. Rose sat down, perched on her chair, back straight.

Pazuzu had four main roads leading into the heart of the city, each positioned like points on a compass. That was no accident. The design was intentional—an open invitation to any traveller, no matter their origin. Whether seeking refuge or simply a place to begin again, all were welcome. Even humans—those few who had turned their backs on the atrocities of their own kind—found a place here.

Over time, this quiet migration became something more. A reconciliation. An understanding. And eventually, recognition: the Commonwealth of NetherKind emerged as a global power and its twelve cities stood as one voice. Humans and NetherKind, once divided, had begun to rebuild a world together. A world now threatening to come undone—over a girl. Over Rose's decision. Over Heidi.

Pazuzu's gate entrances bore names that had lasted centuries: the North Gate, East Passage, Westward Arches, and South Gate. Each led to the city's core, adapting with the times—first carved by foot traffic and horse-drawn carts, then widened and strengthened to bear the weight of the first automobiles.

They didn't align perfectly with true north, south, east or west. But the message was unmistakable: everyone had a way in. Everyone was welcome.

In 1506, when most of the world was still built with timber and hope, Pazuzu raised iron—four gates forged in defiance, shaped by NetherKind hands who understood that survival demanded more than walls. It demanded will.

The Vaylen, with their structural brilliance, engineered the design. The Julpa, their strength unmatched, handled the heaviest loads—lifting, fitting, building. And the Nyssari, ever in tune with the wellbeing of others, saw to every need. They kept the builders nourished, the injured cared for, the spirit of the task alive.

Within six months, Pazuzu rose—not just as the youngest of the NetherKind Cities, but one of the boldest. Built on unity, ingenuity, and the quiet knowledge that it might one day be tested. And it was.

In its six-hundred-year history, the city had only sealed all four roads once. That day, the iron gates—meant to welcome, yet strong enough to withstand—were closed. And they held.

Those same gates still stood, their foundations unchanged. Reinforced, yes, but never replaced. What once symbolised survival had become something quieter. Enduring. Visitors now admired them without understanding their significance. But to those who remembered—or those who cared to learn—they were more than iron and stone.

They were the entrances to the city's arteries. And each one led straight to its heart.

A year later, the English declared war on Pazuzu for aiding Balam—the first NetherKind City—established on the eastern edge of the newly discovered continent, the Americas. Pazuzu shut its gates and the siege began.

For a year, diplomacy faltered. Even Balam's efforts couldn't break the standoff. It wasn't until Malphas, the second NetherKind City, joined the conflict that the tide turned. Together, Malphas and Balam distracted the English forces long enough for Pazuzu to strike. The British stationed outside the gates were overrun and held prisoner for a year within Pazuzu's walls. A ransom note. Let us open the gates and your people will be set free. The siege ended.

It marked the moment the world truly saw what the NetherKind Cities could be. Not fragile enclaves. A force. A network. A united front.

By 1508, Pazuzu reopened its gates. It should have fallen. But it didn't.

And now, Rose stood at the threshold of a decision that might close them again. For the first time in centuries and despite what anyone says about making the right decision, the right decision for some will mean you're on the wrong side of history to others.

Like all NetherKind Cities, Pazuzu established inspection points at every entrance. Though technically within national borders throughout the world, Germany, India, Japan and others, the cities had agreed early in the 20th century to enforce their own checks. Sanctuaries, after all, could be abused.

Yet for those entering Pazuzu, the experience wasn't cold or clinical. The gates no longer stood as stark iron monoliths, but as canvases of colour—painted mosaics danced across their surface, honouring the city's history and those who helped shape it. Bright. Bold. Humble. A welcome with warmth.

But not all cities were as careful.

Rose sat behind her desk once more. To her side, a bowl of fruit sat untouched. A few of the apples were bruising. One of the bananas had begun to spot—dark flecks blooming across its skin like something left too long. It hadn't been like that yesterday. She stared at it for a moment, then pushed the bowl aside. The rot had started. Not just in the fruit. In everything. The outside world was creeping in—through the cracks, under the gates, into her city, into her office, into this.

She exhaled slowly, pulled off her glasses, and pinched the bridge of her nose. The choice itself wasn't hard. It was the weight of it that threatened to crush her. The consequences she couldn't control. She wasn't angry with Heidi. Not really. Just tired. So fucking tired of being the one who always had to explain her, protect her, justify her. And now—now it might cost them everything. If Heidi wasn't in custody by midnight, the Commonwealth could consider Pazuzu complicit. Whether the other NetherKind Cities would stand with them—or turn their backs—added to the uncertainty of what tomorrow would bring. Either way, it looked like war.

Her phone vibrated on the desk, rattling softly against the papers beneath it. She didn't move. Just watched it hum.

It wasn't loud. It wasn't violent.

But it felt like it was.

Then came Adam, cutting across the moment—already holding another phone to his ear, again the mouthpiece was covered.

"I've got Downing Street on the line. They're demanding to speak with you."

Rose raised an eyebrow. "Demanding?"

Adam hesitated. "I, uh… probably shouldn't have said 'demanding.' That was their word."

Her gaze shifted to her personal phone—still vibrating. Still waiting.

She picked it up, then paused. Calm. Decisive.

Without looking at him: "Tell Kenneth I'll call him back when I'm free."

Adam blinked. "Right."

He uncovered the receiver but stalled for a beat, clearly weighing how this would land.

Then, voice a little too careful: "Ms Calloway says she'll return the Prime Minister's call… when she's free."

He didn't wait for a response—just turned and left, a little too quickly. Before she gave him anything more to relay.

Rose pressed the button on her phone. No greeting. Just the three words that had been lodged in her throat all morning:

"Where is she?"

Manchester Orchestra - The Silence

CHAPTER THREE

Fallout

Connor's ears rang. Through the haze, a voice called his name—distant but insistent. Blinking, struggling to focus, he caught blurred shapes moving in a frantic storm around him. People cried out in confusion while others tried to calm them.

He didn't know how long he'd been unconscious. It felt like waking in the wrong place, with no memory of falling asleep—like the world had shifted, and nothing was quite the same.

"Connor! Can you hear me?" The voice again—sharp and familiar.

Connor blinked, struggling to focus. His vision sharpened just enough to catch blurred shapes moving around him. The faint, familiar shimmer of his Vaylen blood pulsed under his skin—bioluminescence flickering where soot didn't cover it—proof he was still breathing, still standing.

"...Yeah. Yeah," he mumbled, as his vision began to sharpen and the fog in his head started to lift. He pushed himself up onto his hands, realising he'd been lying on the floor. A sharp throb pulsed through his skull as blood rushed with the movement.

"I'm okay. I'm good." He was neither.

Connor looked up—the voice belonged to Ellis. He was bent over, hands on his knees, but not in concern. Ellis wasn't at his side checking for injuries or helping him up. Just standing there looking down at him like someone assessing damage rather than a person. His expression was unreadable—hard eyes, tight jaw. No relief, no warmth. Just the bare minimum that it took to confirm Connor was conscious. This wasn't a welfare check. Ellis wasn't here out of concern. He never really had been—not for a long time.

Ellis only wanted to know one thing. And Connor knew, even without being asked. Where was Heidi?

There was no love lost between him and Ellis. But once... once they'd shared something. Not quite friendship, but a connection—tied to someone they both cared about more than themselves.

Ellis offered a hand. Connor took it and was pulled to his feet, the sudden rise making him unsteady. Trying to stay composed, he wobbled and instinctively placed a hand on Ellis's shoulder to steady himself. For a second, both of them stared at the contact—like they'd just broken an unspoken rule. Connor pulled his hand away at once. Falling back on his arse would've been less awkward than touching Ellis.

Conner brushed himself down, shaking soot and gravel from his clothes as his vision steadied and the ground beneath him stopped swaying. Around him, the chaos was beginning to take shape—ambulances and police cars scattered along Pazuzu High Road, the main artery that looped endlessly around the city's edge. It didn't run in one direction but circled the outskirts of the central districts, linking the four gate roads and keeping traffic in constant motion across three lanes each way.

That motion had now stopped.

The roads were frozen in carnage—cars abandoned mid-turn, doors left hanging open. Some had collided, crumpled against each other in tangled heaps of twisted metal. Fires burned in the wreckage, flames licking at the sky through the massive gap in the section of road that was above them—open and exposed.

A section of the overpass had broken away, collapsing onto the road below—the same one Connor now stood on. Though it hadn't completely buckled, deep cracks veined through the tarmac, splitting the surface wide. Beneath his feet, the road gave a low, ominous groan under the added weight. Held together by only the steel girders that were at the core of the concrete.

The swirl of red and blue lights pulsed across the scene, illuminating thick plumes of black smoke as they twisted with the chill Pennine wind. Dust and concrete—flung skyward by the fires—caught in the same current, drifting through the air like ash.

It was a lot to take in.

He shouldn't have survived—he felt that now. And with that realisation came another, colder thought: how many didn't? Did some of the cars still hold bodies? Or what was left of them. Charred remains slumped in the seats—blackened flesh clinging to bone where it hadn't been burned away completely. Those that caught the worst of the explosion. The thought penetrated him.

"Ellis…"

Connor looked around, eyes darting between gurneys and open ambulance doors where paramedics were tending to the injured. Some were being helped by others—people who had also been caught in the chaos but had somehow walked away unscathed.

"How many..?"

The words faltered as panic crept into his voice. The devastation around them was overwhelming, and he was starting to unravel.

Ellis saw it. He stepped in without hesitation, placing both hands firmly on Connor's shoulders, locking eyes with him to centre his focus.

"No one," Ellis said, voice sharp but steady. "No one died."

Connor gasped, the breath catching in his throat finally breaking free.

"Some are hurt worse than others. That's all," Ellis continued.

His calm steadiness grounded Connor just enough and Ellis let go. There was no need to hold Connor steady anymore—the panic had passed.

"Heidi. Where is she?" Ellis asked. There it was. Ellis didn't bother with sincerity or even try to pretend he cared about anything else—he was always straight to the point when it came to Heidi. And in a way, Connor respected that. It wasn't that Ellis was in a rush; he just hated small talk—and, more broadly, people. He'd always been like that, for as long as Connor could remember, back when he, Abi, and Heidi used to hang around The Pit during opening hours after school.

"I don't know where she is. I don't even remember how I got here."

Ellis dealt with customers quickly. Never rude—just… indifferent. He didn't want to hear about anyone's top five drummers or their ten essential desert island discs. Especially not from strangers. But get him talking to Mijo or someone he actually cared about? Then he'd be there for hours—agreeing with you, or more likely, arguing with you about why you were wrong.

Ellis never said much to Connor. He didn't need to as his silence spoke volumes. And yet, the man had given everything for Heidi—his niece.

How Ellis held himself together back then, Connor had no idea. His sister died during childbirth, leaving behind a baby who was half human, half vampire. And just like that, Ellis became her sole guardian. No warning. No preparation. Just a newborn the world wasn't ready for and questions he had no way of answering.

Yeah. It made sense why Ellis had no time for people.

He didn't just put his life on hold—he gave it up. All of it. For someone he'd never asked for, never expected. And still, he gave everything. And still does.

Abi was a given—she and Heidi had been tight since infant school, thick as thieves from the moment they met.

There wasn't a memory Connor had of Heidi that didn't also have Abi in the background somewhere, always orbiting each other, always on the same page. Connor came onto the scene much later, early secondary school. By then, the girls were a unit. But somehow, he found his way in—quietly, gradually. He never quite had their shorthand, never slotted in perfectly, but he was there enough, often enough, to feel like part of the group. Even Ellis seemed to tolerate him. More than that, at times, Connor thought he was getting close. Ellis never said much, but there were moments—shared silences, nods of approval, the odd conversation about music that didn't feel like it was being endured. For a while, Connor believed he was almost in. Almost. Then he started dating Heidi. Then—she'd dumped him. Out of the blue.

It had been almost two—maybe even three—years since she ended it. Officially, it was because he'd started working for Dante. But Connor had never quite believed that was the whole story.

For all her confidence—most of the time worn like armour—there were moments when she questioned why he was with her.

In truth, he often wondered the same. Why was she with him?

The difference was, Connor trusted her. Completely. In everything she said, everything she did.

But that trust hadn't always gone both ways. Even before Dante.

Telling Heidi he loved her hadn't been the way to prove it. But he said it anyway. And he meant it. More than that—he showed it. Or at least, he thought he had. She was always the priority. Always.

It used to be easier—back when they were younger, when she'd show up at his flat in one of Ellis' hoodies she'd 'borrowed' and raid the fridge like she owned the place. They'd have the place to themselves most nights—his mum worked late shifts. She'd crash on his sofa after some gig, head on his shoulder, grumbling about everything and nothing until she fell asleep mid-sentence. She was sharp even then—quicker than anyone, quicker than him—but there was still softness in her edges. They were young, still figuring themselves out—and each other. He'd even lost a few hoodies himself to her

But things changed.

They'd had a fight that was loud and ugly, both of them saying things they didn't mean. She'd turned to walk away and he grabbed her wrist, and asked, "Why do you always have to go it alone?"

Just pure instinct—she dropped him to the floor in one clean move. Her strength and speed were present in the blink of a moment. It was the first time he truly grasped the force that she had been subduing.

She hadn't shouted. Just looked down at him and said, "Because no one else can carry what I have to."

And she was right.

She didn't have to apologise. He shouldn't have grabbed her. That was on him.

But that didn't mean she had to carry it alone anymore. Not now.

Since the breakup, there had been more than a few mornings where they'd woken up next to each other after a night out with shared friends. No blame given. None taken. They never asked who made the first move, or why. It didn't matter. They'd wanted each other's company. That was enough. But enough didn't mean easy. They started to drift with each encounter. As if diluting what they had each time it happened.

"We… I was caught in the explosion." he replied to Ellis. Connor rubbed the back of his neck, blinking against the grit in the air. "Heidi was with Evelyn. And then…"

A low groan rolled beneath their feet—deep, like something straining far below.

"…I woke up with you over me." He glanced at Ellis, trying to gauge his reaction, but Ellis's eyes were fixed on the road ahead.

Another tremor—faint, but enough to rattle loose stones near the curb. Connor shifted his weight.

"I'm sorry—I don't know anything more than that." His voice wavered as he looked around.

"We need to move." Ellis was increasingly aware of their surroundings and ushered Connor to what seemed like a safe horizon in the distance.

"Did she get her?" Connor asked, his words quick now, as if speeding up might outrun what he already sensed. "Did she get Evelyn?"

The smoke was thinning, revealing twisted beams above, the tarmac around them cracked like old skin.

A sharp snap rang out—then the road split beneath them.

No time to react. The ground lurched, sending both Connor and Ells to the tarmac as the structure groaned and gave way with a roar that swallowed everything else.

They scrambled to their feet, no time to think—just run. Behind them, the road continued to fall apart, slabs of concrete dropping in a chorus of destruction. Metal shrieked as a nearby lamppost folded in on itself, vanishing into the smoke.

Just ahead, a parked police car skidded along reluctantly against gravity, tyres shrieking as the road cracked open beneath it. The car veered sideways, clipping a second vehicle—both tore across the fractured tarmac in a scream of metal and glass. One spun out, sliding backwards toward the drop, vanishing with a crunch into the smoke and ruin.

The other teetered—to the right of their path—its headlights stuttering, nose dipping. Then, with a groan of shifting weight, it tipped forward and plunged after the first narrowly missing Ellis.

They didn't stop. Couldn't. The collapse was chasing them now—breaking apart the road behind them with every step.

They didn't slow. Bolted in the opposite direction, toward a group of others who'd reached stable ground, shouting for them to move faster.

They ran uphill against the tilt, lungs tearing, boots slipping on fractured tarmac as the road buckled behind them. Each step was harder than the last—like sprinting up a crumbling wave. The incline steepened. Cracks split wider. Slabs of concrete gave out beneath their heels with sharp, angry snaps.

Almost there.

Ahead, a half-toppled barrier jutted out from the edge—bent but still holding. A possible anchor. Something to grab.

Connor went for it, legs burning, breath ragged. One final stretch. One last leap.

He missed. So did Ellis.

His feet left the ground. For a heartbeat, everything was weightless—air and silence and the sick certainty of falling. Then gravity seized them. The drop wasn't far, but it was steep, jagged, merciless.

Connor's eyes snapped shut. And everything stopped.

A jolt—not pain, not impact. Just… pressure. Firm. Immovable.

He opened one eye.

A massive hand wrapped around his forearm like a steel brace, the grip unshakable. Another held Ellis just as tightly.

They weren't falling anymore. They were rising—lifted without effort, like bags of flour.

Set down. Safe.

Connor's knees buckled as his boots hit solid ground. He turned to see their rescuer step forward, framed by the dust and crumbling edge of the road like he'd walked straight out of the wreckage itself.

The figure stood tall. Broad. Silent.

Soot streaked his bald head and shoulders. Charcoal blackened his arms to the elbow. Across his chest, half-obscured by ash, a faded red AC/DC logo pushed through the grime.

The ground still rumbled beneath them, but he didn't flinch.

Didn't blink.

Didn't move—until he looked down at them, calm and steady.

Mijo.

Even among the Julpa, Mijo stood out—massive, broad, impossible to miss. Two curved horns jutted from his temples, sweeping around his face in an arc that dropped past his chin like a bison's. They were carved with intricate markings—etched symbols and patterns that told the story of his life. Honoured, pivotal, deeply personal moments. Others were traditional, gifted to all Julpa during rites of passage ceremonies as a mark of respect for their tribe.

Mijo wasn't devout in the spiritual practices of his people, but that didn't mean he dismissed them. He believed in the weight of them—the meaning, the history. Whether in the rainforest or the heart of a city, that heritage travelled with him. It was part of who he was.

"Why the fuck were you both stood over there?" Mijo asked, calm as ever.

Despite his size, his voice still carried that soft, warm Hispanic lilt—like he was scolding a pair of kids for playing too close to traffic, not dragging them out of a near-death collapse.

Connor and Ellis doubled over, catching their breath, hearts thudding in their chests.

"Did you not see the massive cracks? Or the crap hanging from up there?" Mijo jabbed a finger toward the overpass above the spot they'd just escaped. As if on cue, one of the dangling girders gave up and slammed into the wreckage below with a crunch.

"See? Literally the worst place you could've stood."

"Yeah, Mijo, we know that now!" Ellis snapped, brushing soot from his arms.

Mijo had a gift for pointing out the obvious, and Ellis had even more of a gift for hating that.

"Thanks, Mijo," Connor said between breaths, more sincere.

Mijo offered a small nod—like saving people was just part of the day.

Ellis straightened up, eyes scanning the chaos again. "Any signs?" he asked.

"I've checked everywhere. Under everything. She's not here.

Mijo paused, his voice tight with optimism.

She's alive though. I heard someone telling the police that a girl with black and white hair was darting all over the place, getting everyone to safety.

Heidi for sure."

For someone usually so upbeat—always the first to make light of a situation—Mijo's solemn demeanour weighed heavily on him "Though...they said she was pretty beaten up."

At eighty-four, Mijo was closer to Pop-Pop's age than the others, though among the Julpa, he was still considered young-ish. In human terms, he and Ellis, who had recently turned forty-four much to his own annoyance, were roughly the same age in terms of life expectancy.

Mijo had grown up in a large tribal village nestled deep in the South American rainforest, about a two-day walk from Sachamama—the only NetherKind City to rise in South America. Hidden in the heart of the Brazilian jungle, Sachamama was as protected by nature as it was by its people. Those who made the journey were greeted with warmth, music, and open arms. And Mijo was the living embodiment of this Sachamama tradition.

Meeting Ellis while working as a customs guard at the Pazuzu border changed Mijo's life—especially when he was introduced to newborn Heidi. At the time, Ellis was seeking refuge, pursued by the British police for simply trying to protect his niece. Pazuzu offered sanctuary, and Mijo was the first to welcome them in.

He took particular satisfaction in stopping the police cold—reminding them, with a grin, that they had no jurisdiction beyond the gates. From that moment on, Mijo made sure Ellis and Heidi crossed into the city without issue.

Officially, he was let go not long after—for "failing to follow protocol." Unofficially, everyone knew he'd bent the rules. But Mijo never saw it as a failure. He'd let Ellis and Heidi into his life, given them a chance. And if that was a mistake, he'd make it again. Every time.

Over the years, Mijo bonded deeply with Heidi—and Ellis welcomed it. It gave him a much-needed break now and then, and he trusted Mijo completely. But Mijo's time with Heidi was spent very differently than Ellis's.

Where Ellis provided structure and protection, Mijo brought curiosity—and a playful edge. Knowing Heidi was capable of more than most kids, the two of them began running informal "tests" to explore her limits. It started innocently enough: how fast she could run, how far she could jump, what she could lift. But that quickly got boring.

So the tests evolved—more creative, more ambitious, increasingly... unorthodox. Each one pushed her a little further. Not out of cruelty, but fascination. Wonder. They weren't trying to break her. They were trying to understand her. Mijo's Julpa resilience—tough skin and all—meant he could offer a kind of protection no one else could. And the "tests" continued evolving more into an episode of Jackass with each new entry.

Pazuzu City had become Mijo's adopted home, with Ellis and Heidi now part of his chosen family. Now, as he looked around, everything was burning—it felt like it was all falling apart before his eyes.

"I heard someone being interviewed by one of the cops." Mijo said.

"Heidi saved a lot of people, Ellis. Like a lot, lot!" There was excitement and pride in his voice. "Do you think they'll still be after her?"

Mijo put a lot of trust in Ellis. Their bond had formed fast, grounded in a shared love of rock music. Together, they'd built The Pit—a live venue by night, a record store by day. A clever idea, sure, but it was their sheer passion for music that made it work. It wasn't just a business. It became a home. A place for Ellis and Mijo to build something real. A place for Heidi, Abi, and Connor to grow up.

"I don't know Mijo, if it stops all this shit going on then yeah. Which means we need to find her before they do."

Ellis gestured towards a police officer that was mid interview with a bystander, also trying to piece together what had happened. "We're out of time and after this…" Ellis looked at the surroundings, "They'll hand her over without hesitation."

"But this was all Evelyn!" Connor said.

"Who we also need to find. There's no way I'm letting her pin this shit on Heidi."

Connor watched the smoke roll down the street, curling low through the fractured light. Firefighters and police barked instructions, urging people back—now, quick, behind the line. There was no shouting for control, just clear, practiced urgency. Small chunks of concrete pattered down from the overpass above, scattering across the road like grit shaken from the sky.

Connor glanced between the two beside him—Ellis, wound tight and ready to move; Mijo, still and watchful, scanning the haze like he could hear something the rest of them couldn't.

Connor felt like he'd missed something while unconscious. The three of them were here trying to figure out how to help Heidi—when maybe, she'd already made that decision herself.

"This is bollocks."

Ellis turned to him, eyebrows raised—half surprise, half warning. Connor didn't back off.

"You want to protect her?" he said. "Then we do it right. We don't just throw her in a van and hope it sorts itself out. Not after everything."

He paused.

"Whatever she's done… whatever she's stuck in—she didn't run. She stood her ground. She made the call. We back her. Yeah?"

Silence.

Mijo gave a slow, quiet nod.

Ellis's jaw tightened. He looked at Connor like he wanted to push back—but didn't.

Connor turned toward the road, still broken, still smouldering.

Somewhere out there, Heidi was bleeding. Whether she wanted help or not.

Ellis' phone buzzed—a sharp vibration cutting through the chaos. He usually ignored such notifications, preferring to check them later. He wasn't one to be tethered to his screen like so many others. But now, with everything unravelling and the possibility that it was Heidi, he reached into the lower leg pocket of his cargo trousers and unlocked the screen.

James had sent him a message.

A flicker of relief crossed his face.

He looked up at Mijo and Connor.

"I know where she is," he said.

REO Speedwagon - Don't Let Him Go

CHAPTER FOUR

Pop-Pop

The tonearm was moved with grace and care into position above the spinning vinyl. With his index finger steady against the cartridge, Pop-Pop lined up the stylus, releasing the locked mechanism with a surgeon's touch. He took the weight of the tonearm, lowered it slowly, and let the needle kiss the black vinyl. Then—he let go.

A crackle of static snapped from the speakers, cutting through the quiet. A heartbeat later, the low hum of a guitar rolled out— followed by drums, steady and deliberate. The sound filled the room slowly, seeping into every corner, every crack in the old plaster and worn floorboards. The Pit didn't just carry music—it remembered it. It had soaked it in for years, through every gig, every soundcheck, every band that had ever stood on its stage. Music lived here. It resonated in the bones of the building, in the mismatched tiles and battered stools, in the faded posters that still clung to the walls like loyal ghosts. The moment that first note hit, something shifted—like the venue itself exhaled. It wasn't just sound anymore, The Pit was awake.

Grinning, Pop-Pop gave his hips a defiant shake, dancing with a pint in hand like a man who'd earned the right to move however he pleased. He shuffled into the rhythm, beer sloshing gently in one hand, the other keeping loose time against his leg. This was how you warmed a place up. This was how you reminded the walls they were still alive.

For once, he had the place to himself. No customers. No noise but the music. No one around to see how much slower he moved these days. Heidi had been pulled into something he couldn't dream of keeping up with. Fit and sprightly for seventy-four or not, he'd have been nothing but a hindrance.

Ellis and Mijo had gone after her—just as he would have, once.

The truth was, he felt useless. Helpless.

So he did the only thing he could.

He put some music on. And drank.

Maybe a little too much.

Pop-Pop bopped over to his usual stool, carefully balancing his beer, and dropped himself into his favourite seat. The muted TV on the wall flickered to his left, rolling through the live news.

He'd thought about heading out on his motorcycle—a custom chopper almost the size of a small car—but that was useless now. No way to navigate through a city locked in chaos.

No, best to stay put, quietly worry, and have a drink.

The Pit was more than familiar. It was a home away from home. They all joked he spent more time here than at his actual flat, and it was probably true. What would he have done at home anyway? Sit and watch daytime TV?

At least here, he could drink a proper pint and watch the real world pass him by—not some fictional soap hospital or made-up neighbourhood drama.

He did have a soft spot for kids' cartoons, though. At least they were entertaining.

On the muted TV screen, a breaking news ticker crawled across the bottom: "Heidi Evervale, the vampire hybrid at the centre of Pazuzu's 2003 controversy, is now linked to today's citywide disruption."

Muted. It was always muted.

This was a record store. Music came first.

Right now, REO Speedwagon's "Don't Let Him Go" was just kicking in, filling The Pit with its raw guitars and urgent beat.

The TV wasn't really there for the news anyway. Its real job was to display the menu and pricing for the coffee shop—a small section tucked off to the right as you entered The Pit, called 'Brew-hemian Rhapsody', where Pop-Pop now sat. Named by yours truly. A peaceful little settlement away from the endless aisles that filled the store, stretching out with miles of vinyl.

Behind the main counter, a wide staircase fanned out at the bottom and narrowed as it rose, leading up to the staff-only area—home to the kitchen, Ellis's office, and all the other junk they didn't have a better place for.

The building itself dated back to the 1950s. Ellis and Mijo had fallen in love with it the moment they saw it—drawn to the character and history etched into every wall, every floorboard. It had good bones, and even better potential. Instead of stripping it back or modernising it into something sterile, they leaned into its roots—embracing the era with dulled-out pinks, off-whites, and just enough neon to give it a heartbeat. The place was well lit by hanging Cornetto lights that cast a soft, inviting glow across the shop floor. It wasn't just a record store. It wasn't just a venue. It was a home—for them, and for anyone else who needed it.

Downstairs, the basement had been transformed into a live music venue. Neither Ellis nor Mijo knew the first thing about proper DIY, and the early attempts showed it. There was quite literally blood in the concrete from accidents involving hammers, drills, and more enthusiasm than skill. But somehow, that made it better. Real. On a good night, packed to capacity with 300 bodies, the sweat dripped from the low ceiling as the crowd packed the floor, singing in unison to their favourite bands—every voice, every stomp, every note hammered into the walls. It wasn't polished. It wasn't perfect. But it was theirs. And it belonged to anyone else that wanted to enjoy it.

When Pop-Pop first turned up at Pazuzu, he could have wept at the state of the basement. It wasn't horrendous—but it was far from perfect. Without apology, he chucked Ellis and Mijo out, handed them a list of supplies, and gave one instruction: leave it all by the door and stay the hell out. For three days, no one was allowed in. No one except Heidi.

It was the first time they'd really spent any time together. She'd only just been introduced to him—barely five years old, all wide eyes and wary silences. But something clicked. Pop-Pop worked. Heidi watched. He'd talk—endlessly—about the bands he'd toured with, the chaos of life on the road, the moments that stuck with him. Stories not always fit for younger ears, but he regularly forgot that, getting carried away in the rhythm of it all. Heidi didn't seem to mind. She sat there, besotted, passing him tools when he called them out, getting most of them right, some hilariously wrong. At times, despite her age, even then her strength helped him lift when he'd struggled.

There was no plan to it, no big gesture. Just the beginning of something real—quietly built between songs, stories, and sawdust. For Pop-Pop—who missed his chance with Nina and Ellis as kids—it was more than he'd ever expected.

All Ellis and Mijo could do was listen from upstairs—three days sound testing and adjusting of drums, guitars, keys, and a lot of colourful swearing echoing through the mics. More than a few customers asked what the hell was going on down there. Truth was, Ellis and Mijo were wondering the same.

On the third day, Pop-Pop finally emerged, sweaty, tired, but grinning like a man who knew he'd nailed it. His only instruction: don't touch a single fucking thing. Which Heidi echoed word for word. Pop-Pop had made an impression that was for sure.

The sound was crisp, clean—provided the soundchecks were done properly. During the smaller, more intimate gigs, the room was tuned so finely you could hear a needle drop between songs. Pop-Pop had done his job—and he'd done it well.

Five listening booths lined the wall behind Brewhemian Rhapsody, where customers could buy a drink and test out an LP before deciding whether to take it home.

A slightly archaic way to find new music, especially with all the streaming services available—but people liked it. Ellis said it was because it felt more connected, more intimate to the music.

Pop-Pop didn't argue back which was his way of agreeing.

The coffee shop had been a late addition, introduced a few months after The Pit first opened. The booths, though, had been there since day one—and were getting more use than Ellis liked back in the early days. Customers would grab a record, sit down, listen through… then just put it back. Few bought.

The coffee shop idea had sparked when Ellis noticed people bringing in outside drinks—or worse, food—then settling into a booth for a 40-minute chill session. At first, he let it slide. But the mess—crumbs, takeaway packaging, spilled drinks—got under his skin. So, he flipped it.

If people wanted drinks, they'd get drinks—from The Pit. The introduction of a proper drinks menu - coffee, tea, hot chocolate and an assortment of fizzy drinks, gave The Pit a financial boost, and customers loved it. So much so, Ellis took it a step further. There was an alcohol license for the venue bar downstairs, so Ellis made the most of it. He added alcohol to the menu. Craft beer. Cider on tap. A few solid draught pumps. No "carbonated shite," as Ellis called the fizzy swill served in regular pubs. Again, Pop-Pop didn't argue.

Pop-Pop's visits, which had once been every other week to see his son and granddaughter, soon became weekly. Then a few times a week. Then… every day.

He'd come to Pazuzu reluctantly at first, but the place grew on him fast. He and Ellis had never truly got on—but Heidi… well, Heidi was his only grandchild. And after everything, he felt he owed Nina that much. Considering both she and Ellis had grown up with barely a father, the least he could do now was show up.

Being a roadie meant being on tour. Always. One band's tour would end, and another would start—and he'd be right there, back on the road. The '70s were a blur—most of it lost in the haze of drugs and booze that seemed to flow endlessly from town to town. Fans were generous, too often all it took was a backstage pass in exchange for a bottle or a bump. Jimi, Led Zep, Elton… it'd be quicker to list the bands he hadn't toured with.

When Ellis and then Nina were born, people told him it was time to slow down. Buckle up. Be a dad. But instead, he doubled down—threw himself even harder into life on the road. Avoiding responsibility? Yeah. He was good at that.

Grace was left to do all the heavy lifting, and whatever excuse they had for a relationship finally wore thin.

As Ellis and Nina got older, he saw less and less of them. They were busy, growing up, doing their own thing—like kids do. And him? He was the one being left behind. Especially when he found out Ellis had started drumming. Was even in a band. It should've been the perfect excuse to reconnect. But Ellis? He was either too busy—or just didn't want to hear it.

Nina was different. She never let him off the hook—not even when she was little.

She was relentless—for all of them. Always the bridge between broken pieces.

While Ellis was off touring sold-out arenas with Mavis Deacon & The Renegades, Nina was working a bar in Manchester, staying close to Grace. And she kept Ellis grounded. You could see the fame creeping in, but Nina? She'd snap him right back down to Earth.

Then, she got pregnant.

Twenty-years old—younger than he'd been when she and Ellis were born.

He'd never seen her so content.

Not in that smug, gloating way some expectant mums carried themselves.

Nina didn't let the pregnancy slow her down; she just got on with it. She was simply... happy.

By then, Grace had already passed away.

Her last few years had been spent with someone else—someone who made her happy. Someone who deserved her.

Pop-Pop, meanwhile, had sunk deeper into the bottle than ever before, drowning in the feeling that he'd failed—as a father and as a partner.

Neither he nor Grace had ever been the marrying type.

Old hippies, both of them, who thought the bond they shared was enough.

Or so they believed.

It was Nina who pulled him back—just in time—before he hit bottom.

She helped him find the balance he needed.

He knew she had done the same for Ellis too.

As for Nina's guy?

He never found out who he was. Neither did Ellis.

They'd asked her once—together—the day she told them she was expecting.

She'd just smiled and said:

"She's got who she needs," Nina said with a crooked grin. "One of you's never held a baby, and the other only started turning up when I could hold a pint."

Ellis gave a small huff of a laugh, looking down. Pop-Pop grunted, not quite offended—but not disagreeing either.

They didn't argue. They couldn't.

It was never mentioned again. Not when Nina was around, anyway.

Then—the happiest day became the worst.

Nina died during childbirth. Heidi arrived, and Nina was gone. To Pop-Pop's surprise, Ellis gave up everything. The band. The tours. The dream. He stepped into guardianship in a way Pop-Pop never had. And though it was never said aloud, Pop-Pop knew: Ellis had done what he hadn't.

And maybe… maybe that was enough.

There was no point trying to prove anything anymore. At first, he'd been angry—furious at the world. But he understood: this time, putting up walls wasn't going to help anyone.

They needed to grieve, sure—but more than that, they needed to protect Heidi.

Raise her. Together.

When the headlines about Heidi hit—and the threats followed—they had to disappear. Fast. They decided that Ellis should go with Heidi. Pop-Pop could then handle the press, the police, the politicians. The Three P's, Ellis and Pop-Pop had named them. Pop-Pop would join them when everything calmed down. If it calmed down.

Pazuzu City became their refuge. A chance to start again. A place where even the NetherKind offered support. And this time, Pop-Pop stayed. Neither of them had a clue how to raise a baby—let alone a vampire baby. Mijo knew even less. But that didn't matter. They figured it out. Somehow.

The bond between him and Ellis was different from what he'd had with Nina. The two of them were too alike, which meant they knew exactly how to get on each other's nerves. Still, they persevered. And eventually, they built something—not quite a friendship, not quite a father-son thing. Just their own version of it.

And most days…it worked.

Ellis even let him pick the draught lineup.

Pop-Pop became The Pit's unofficial barman—a role he gladly accepted, paid entirely in beer. A retired roadie with a lifetime of stories, he was always happy to share tales from his days on tour with bands like The Rolling Stones and a long list of others most people had never heard of—but which, to him, mattered more than the big names ever could.

He'd perch himself at the end of the bar, always within arm's reach of the pump for easy top-ups. It was his spot. His stage.

Pop-Pop had a real knack for storytelling. Even the dullest anecdote came to life when filtered through his encyclopaedic knowledge of rock music and the people who made it.

Sometimes, he'd even get customers to pour their own pints—usually ending in a bad pour, too much foam, less beer used… more profit. Ellis had no complaints.

Except, of course, when someone actually asked for coffee.

That's when Ellis or Heidi would step in.

There were no customers right now.

Pop-Pop finished his beer, reached over the bar, and pulled himself another with the kind of ease that only came from habit and repetition.

His granddaughter was in trouble. His son was out there, somewhere in the chaos. And him? He was no help to either of them. Too old. Too slow. Useless.

"Are you open?"

The voice made Pop-Pop jolt so hard he nearly toppled off his stool.

"JESUS!" he barked, spilling half his drink as he scrambled to steady himself.

He twisted around, heart thumping harder than he'd like to admit, and found a woman standing just inside the entrance doorway to The Pit.

"What the fuck—you can't just sneak up on an old man like that!" he said, half-laughing, half-growling.

"Sorry," she said, smiling. "The door was open."

"Yeah, forgot to lock it," he muttered, grabbing a cloth to mop up the mess. "Guess that means we're open. For now."

"Perfect." She smiled wider and drifted toward the rows of records.

Pop-Pop shook his head, grumbling under his breath as he mopped up the worst of the spill.

He wiped down his stool, refilled his pint properly this time, set the dripping rag aside, and shuffled back over to the record player behind the counter. As he moved, Pop-Pop glanced over at the new customer.

Well put together for a place like The Pit, he thought—but then again, it didn't take much to outshine the usual crowd.

She looked no older than forty, with a kind of natural beauty that didn't feel forced.

It was as if Audrey Hepburn had come up through the mid-'90s grunge scene—grown up, roughened at the edges, but still carrying that effortless grace.

That kind of look where it seemed like she hadn't tried at all... and somehow, that made it even better.

In her case, it was stunning.

The world was falling to pieces outside, and here she was—hunting for vinyl.

If he didn't have people he cared about out there in the thick of it, he might've admired her for it.

"You just browsing?" he called over his shoulder as he lifted the needle from the spinning LP. The music came to a halt.

"Yeah," she said, her voice warm, casual.

"Just seeing what treasures I can find."

She ran her fingers lightly along the spines of the records as she moved through the aisles, pausing now and then to flick through a few.

Pop-Pop let her wander, setting the old record aside and reaching for another.

It was the first slice of normal he'd seen all day.

After a few minutes, she spoke again, almost offhand.

"Been chasing my holy grail for a while now."

Pop-Pop turned, distracted from the sleeve he was holding.

"Oh yeah? What's that?"

She glanced over her shoulder at him, smiling.

"Bootleg. Deep Purple. Made in Japan. Original pressing."

Now that made him stand up a little straighter.

Specific. Old-school. A woman with proper taste.

"You'll be hard pressed to find that," he said dryly.

She chuckled. "Good one."

Pop-Pop let out a grunt that could almost pass for a laugh.

Still flicking through the 'D' section, she paused, frowning, flicked back to 'C,' then back to 'D,' squinting at the labels.

"You know these aren't in alphabetical order, right?" she called.

Pop-Pop smirked into his pint.

"Yeah, that's Mijo's doing. No one finds shit unless he's in. You just gotta search and hope for the best."

She shook her head, amused, but didn't seem put off.

"I kind of like that," she said. "Makes it feel like... I dunno. Like the records pick you."

Pop-Pop raised his glass to that.

Wasn't about to argue with someone who respected a little chaos.

"You want a drink?" he offered, more out of habit than anything else. "World's ending, after all."

She hesitated, then glanced toward the towering front windows that spanned both floors of The Pit. The upper level, open and overlooking the bustling lower floor, offered a panoramic view of the city beyond. Far off, a low plume of smoke drifted above the rooftops—soft, grey, almost serene at this distance. She watched it for a moment, unreadable, then shrugged like it was nothing.

"Why not."

Pop-Pop jerked his thumb toward the bar taps.

"Help yourself."

She blinked, caught off guard.

"Seriously?"

"Dead serious," he said with a shrug. "End times. House rules."

She grinned then, tension breaking, made her way behind the bar. A few moments later, she'd poured a pint with a steady hand.

Pop-Pop gave a satisfied grunt.

"Now that's the kind of survivor we need more of."

The woman came around to the front of the counter, pint in hand, and leaned against it casually.

"I was there, you know," Pop-Pop casually bragged. "In Japan. When they recorded it."

"Wait—seriously? You were there? In the crowd?" Now he had her attention, a clue perhaps to the treasured LP she was searching for? She lay her pint down in front of his, like two mates catching up.

"No. I was the roadie."

"No kidding?" He placed the needle on the new LP that he had set up and turned back to face her.

"Yep." The Outside by A Perfect Circle started to play on the speakers. Loud like before. Pop-Pop turned it down so they could at least speak without yelling over it.

On the muted TV now in the background, flames and footage of the city's chaos rolled on. Pop-Pop ignored it. Same headlines, different phrasing. Right now, this was better. It was a welcome distraction. He turned to face the woman, her in front of the counter, him behind, both with a beer in hand.

"There's a brief moment on the original pressing," he said as she sipped from the glass, locking eyes on him as he spoke. A willing audience for once. He continued, "Ritchie accidentally unhooks his guitar from the amp—still don't know how. But you can hear the static and feedback when I plug it back in. Before they cleaned it up, anyway."

"He stepped on it," the woman said casually, placing her glass back on the counter and wiping her lips to ensure there was no beer-tache.

"He stepped on it?" Pop-Pop knew this story. He told it a thousand times and knew it backwards. Not once had he ever been corrected.

"The guitar wire… or whatever you call it. He stepped on it." She raised her pint, eyes still locked on Pop-Pop. "Wonder whose fault that was?" she added with a smile—

knowing full well it was probably the roadie who hadn't handed the cable off properly. She took another sip

"Lead. Guitar lead." His tone had changed. That wasn't common knowledge. That moment had never been written down, never repeated. Only the crew knew it. And this woman wasn't even born in '72.

He looked at her carefully. "I'm Pop-Pop."

"Is that your real name?" she laughed, placing her glass back on the counter. Pop-Pop snickered.

"You know sometimes I forget, it's what everyone calls me."

She extended her hand and took Pop-Pop's hand.

"Well Pop-Pop. Nice to meet you. I'm Evelyn. Evelyn Shaw."

The air shifted. Something about the conversation had suddenly made everything feel different—her knowing smile, her calm—and the fangs that her smile had revealed now that they were up close. A subtle pink hue lingered around the irises too, faint but unmistakable. He hadn't noticed them before—too caught up in the banter, the dim lighting, the normalcy of it all. But now, up close, with her eyes fixed on him, there was no missing it.

He inhaled, as if he'd just been plunged neck deep into ice water.

Pop-Pop gave a small nod as they let go of each other's grasp. "Thought so."

He'd been in hundreds of dangerous situations before and talked himself out of them. This was no different.

He glanced toward the muted TV, then back to her. "So now what?"

He knew the danger she posed. But the nerve of her, walking into The Pit like this—calm, casual, boots on the floor of his place like it meant nothing. He didn't know whether to admire it or call it plain stupid. He guessed he would decide after he saw the outcome. If he saw it.

The only thing, why was Evelyn Shaw, the woman Heidi, Ellis and Mijo were after, why was she here? With him.

"We finish our pints?" Evelyn suggested.

Pop-Pop took a slow sip.

Savouring it like it might be his last.

R.E.M. - Leave

CHAPTER FIVE

A Knock at the Gates

The city had come to a standstill.

If you weren't on foot, you were stuck—trapped on one of Pazuzu City's main roads, gridlocked with no end in sight. Even those trying to enter the city had ground to a halt outside the gates. The tram system, which usually weaved through and above the city connecting outer neighbourhoods to the central zones, had also shut down. A section of track had collapsed completely from the blast—lines now left dangling, bent and twisted, with hundreds stranded between stations.

Outside each of Pazuzu's four gates, the British Army had established a visible and deliberate presence. What began as a small contingent had grown steadily over the past forty-eight hours—one unit per gate, rifles slung, faces unreadable, all waiting for the order no one wanted to give. Yesterday, tanks had rolled in and taken up position just behind the front lines—their arrival loud, unmistakable, and impossible to ignore.

Officially, nothing had changed. The gates remained open. The roads were still accessible. Diplomats talked in circles. Commanders waited for orders that weren't coming. And inside the city, tension thickened. Troop numbers had doubled. Their presence wasn't just strategic anymore—it was a warning, loud and looming.

To the troops stationed outside, it still felt like theatre. No one truly believed they'd be ordered to breach Pazuzu's gates—not without igniting a war. The idea wasn't just unthinkable. It was untenable.

Yet ironically, the gridlocked traffic was the most activity they'd seen in days. And for Brigadier Philip Locke, it was the first disruption worth noticing—the first ripple in a stagnant standoff.

Officially, their presence was part of a peaceful transfer—an escort to ensure Heidi Evervale's safe handover. That's how it had been framed. Quiet. Controlled. Cooperative.

Unofficially, there was a second mandate. One not printed or spoken of—just understood: if diplomacy failed, they would go in, locate the girl, and extract her by force.

Air support couldn't be stationed nearby. The jagged terrain of the Pennines made that impossible. But two helicopters sat ready on a flat plain just beyond the ridge—out of sight, close enough to deploy within minutes.

They'd been waiting for two days. The message from above had been unambiguous: any attempt to seize Heidi by force would risk war. So they waited—boots planted, weapons ready, eyes on the gates.

Diplomatic channels were all but drained. Midnight was the deadline. Four hours to go.

What was causing the delay, Locke didn't know. No updates. No movement. Just orders—and silence.

The Pazuzu gates remained open, which meant diplomacy hadn't failed. Not yet.

Inside the field tent just beyond the North Gate, Locke paced in silence—patience thinning, same as the rest of the world.

Heidi Evervale had always been a problem. Not to him personally and not for what she'd done, but for what she was. From the moment of her birth, she was an unknown—a living contradiction the world had no framework for. And with the unknown came fear.

Everyone remembered the headlines: the first human–vampire hybrid, born right here in the UK. But it wasn't just news—it was debate, hysteria, it was ancient myths reborn. A potential new species of NetherKind. Half vampire, no less. And vampires hadn't been truly seen—not openly—since the Ash Dawn, a dark chapter humanity still hadn't forgiven itself for.

What did Heidi represent? A fluke? A new evolution? A one-off... or the start of something more? A super-species born from one of the most powerful bloodlines in NetherKind history?

Vampires were not to be underestimated. Aside from the Julpa, they were physically the strongest of the NetherKind species—and they healed fast. Far faster than any human ever could. The old myths—that they fed on humans, drank us dry? Lies.

The truth was much quieter. Vampires lived off the land—livestock, stored blood, often needing just a single animal per month, per vampire. Sustainable and hidden, it was myth turned mundane.

Of all the NetherKind, vampires had proven the least threatening. But they were few, scattered, and largely nomadic. Locke had read about hidden colonies living in cave systems, well off the map. One, he was certain, existed far to the north—Norway, maybe—where the nights stretched endlessly at certain times of the year.

Sunlight still killed them. So did decapitation. So did a stake through the heart. However, Locke had always figured those were more general rules for everyone than just vampire-specific ones.

He didn't recall much from school history, but he remembered the shame—the quiet, national shame—that came from nearly wiping out an entire species over lies and fear. Even after centuries the guilt hadn't eroded.

And yet... if Heidi herself hadn't been dangerous when she was born, what had changed? What had she done to bring the world to the edge of war?

Locke's unit was positioned close enough to respond if things turned ugly, but not so close as to spark immediate escalation. That was the theory. In practice, it meant being parked in full view of a city that clearly wanted them gone.

On day one, Pazuzu's Garrison had begun quietly patrolling the upper walkways of the North Gate—a silent show of force that hadn't gone unnoticed. And from what Locke had over the radio, the same slow standoff was playing out at every gate.

Two sides. Each waiting. Each watching. Ready to react the moment the other made a move.

"Those little shits—look at them."

Amy, one of Locke's troops, nodded toward the stalled traffic beyond the gate.

Earlier in the day, it had been a steady stream—cars, trucks, tourist buses creeping forward, drivers glaring through windows as they passed. But now everything was frozen. Right in front of them sat a school bus, stuck mid-turn on the outer road, full of kids returning from a field trip.

One of them, no older than twelve, was pressed against the glass. Middle finger raised. Expression blank. Like it was his duty.

Locke didn't blink.

"Ignore them," he said evenly. "Just kids being kids."

It was unfortunate, having to be this close to the gates—but it was necessary. If something flared up, they had to be ready to mobilise within minutes, even if it meant clashing with the gate guards. Still, marching into Pazuzu uninvited would be seen not just as aggression against the city itself, but as an act of war against all twelve NetherKind Cities. That fact had been made painfully clear to him—more than once.

And so they waited.

Locke wondered if the other units were putting up with the same shit at their gates. Probably. Still, he radioed the South Gate—less for intel, more just to break the monotony.

"South Gate, this is North. You getting the same traffic chaos we are?"

A burst of static, then a reply.

"Yep. Total gridlock. Word is the ring road's out. Same story at West and East.

"Copy that," Locke muttered.

The steady blare of car horns from beyond the ridge drilled into Locke's skull—long, frustrated bursts rising and falling like waves. Past the checkpoint, the smarter drivers had abandoned their seats, stepping out into the shoulder of the road where the overgrown shrubbery encroached like a slow tide. Coats were tied around waists, bottles of water passed between hands. People milled about in small pockets, some pacing, others perched on bonnets, trying to make the best of a bad situation. One family had taken things a step further—

clearing a patch of gravel to kick a football around. The father stood in the makeshift goal, arms outstretched, while his kids darted through scattered tufts of grass and roadside litter, shrieking with laughter. It had the feel of a reluctant picnic. A forced pause no one wanted but everyone was learning to endure.

One of the kids—a young Vaylen, no older than ten—got a little too ambitious with his kick. The ball soared off his foot, bounced once, then slammed into the side of a nearby car that clearly didn't belong to the family. A dull thud rang out.

The driver's door burst open. A Julpa, broad-shouldered and already scowling, clambered out with enough force to make the entire car creak. He pointed a thick, accusing finger at the child and stormed across the tarmac, each heavy step crunching gravel beneath him.

"Watch where you're kicking that fucking ball, you little dick!"

Locke, watching from the tent, arched an eyebrow but didn't move. The outburst wasn't unexpected—tensions were high, patience thin.

Before the Julpa could get closer, the boy's father stepped in—calm, quick, deliberate. A hand on his son's shoulder, a steady voice raised just enough to be heard. "Apologies. He didn't mean it. We'll put the ball away."

No anger. No defensiveness. Just quiet authority and a refusal to escalate. Locke noted the way the father stood—shoulders back, gaze steady but non-threatening. A practiced peacekeeper. Or maybe just a parent who'd defused too many fights already that day.

Locke watched from the tent, jaw tight. The Julpa was clearly spoiling for an argument, but the kid? He'd barely scuffed the paint. The suspension was already gone—he could hear it when the driver got out. One more knock wouldn't have changed anything.

Still, the Julpa wasn't letting it drop. Whether it was cabin fever from hours spent stewing in gridlock or just the fact that the man was, in Locke's professional opinion, a world-class bellend, the result was the same. He paced in tight, aggressive steps, eyes wide with performative outrage.

"Sorry? He could've smashed the window with me still in the car—then what?!"

Locke let out a short, quiet scoff. As if the worst-case scenario was a glancing blow turning his window into a hailstorm of glass. This wasn't a threat from the Julpa—it was a tantrum dressed up in his own logic. He'd seen Julpa take a round to the chest and keep moving. This was theatre. Nothing more.

The Vaylen father didn't rise to it. He stood steady, one hand still resting on his son's shoulder, his voice calm. "Sir, I've already apologised. We'll stop playing—just in case."

No sarcasm. No fear. Just quiet control.

"Are you threatening me now?" the Julpa snapped, voice rising.

"What? No! I—"

"'Just in case'? What's that supposed to mean?!"

He stepped closer—looming now, using every inch of his size to press the point. No fists, no yelling. Just posture. Classic intimidation. Locke had seen it a hundred times—different uniforms, same tactic.

That was enough.

He passed his rifle off to Amy without a word and started across the grass.

"Hey!"

His voice cracked through the tension—sharp, level, and unmistakably military.

The Julpa froze. Eyes turned. Conversations stalled. Even the ball lay still where it had rolled against the tyre of a car.

A few nearby drivers who had stepped out to stretch their legs paused mid-step. A mother holding her child turned instinctively toward the noise. For the moment, the standoff became the only thing happening.

Locke advanced with calm purpose, every footstep pressing down the wild tufts of grass that divided the road from the field encampment. The distance wasn't far, but with every stride, he felt the weight of eyes. Observing. Judging. Not just the Julpa—but him.

An outsider walking into someone else's tension. Someone else's city.

"The guy said sorry," Locke continued, approaching at a steady pace. "It's done. No harm, no foul."

He raised both hands—palms out, unarmed, nothing provocative. The kind of posture that said, I'm not here to fight… unless you are.

Up close, the Julpa was even bigger than he'd looked from the tent. Solid. Towering. A wall in boots.

Locke came to a stop in front of the Julpa, the line of stalled traffic stretching behind him, the towering iron gates rising beyond the Julpa's shoulder. The symbolism wasn't lost on him—an outsider stepping between two locals, flanked by the steel edge of a city that didn't want him here. But before he could speak again, the boy's father stepped forward—not aggressive, but firm.

"It's handled," he said calmly, placing a steady hand on Locke's arm—not to challenge, but to redirect. "No harm done, no need for escalation."

His voice still, even. "I appreciate the concern, but this was just a misunderstanding. We've got it."

There was nothing confrontational in his tone—no raised voice, no hostility. But the message was clear enough: You're not needed here. Not in this moment. Definitely not in this city.

The Julpa bore down, ready for a fight. Locke squared up, on his tiptoes—not backing off, not giving ground.

The Julpa sneered, voice low but venomous.

"This your job now? Bark at civilians to make yourself feel taller?"

Locke didn't flinch.

"And yours is what—screaming at kids? Or picking on someone who isn't three feet shorter than you?"

The Julpa stepped closer, nostrils flaring. "Careful, soldier. You don't get to throw your weight around here."

Locke matched his tone, cold and steady. "Neither do you."

Before the Julpa could respond, a voice cut through from the side—one of the drivers leaning against a bonnet, arms folded.

"Maybe try minding your own business for once, yeah?"

For a second, Locke assumed it was aimed at the Julpa. Then he caught the look—pointed, unblinking—and realised the comment was aimed at him.

A murmur of agreement rippled through the others nearby. Not loud. But enough. The tension in the air changed—heavier, more watchful. It wasn't just about the argument anymore. It was about who belonged here.

Locke held his ground, jaw tight. He glanced around—not in fear, but in recognition. This wasn't his space. Not really. No matter the uniform.

And the city knew it. And it was right.

The Vaylen father stepped in again—gentle but clear, his voice steady as he turned slightly toward Locke.

"Look, I appreciate the intention," he said. "But things are calm now. Best not to let it flare up again. Probably wiser for everyone if you let it be."

No challenge. Just quiet reasoning. A way out without humiliation.

Locke gave a short nod.

Not retreat. Just… awareness.

Then he turned and walked back toward the tent—shoulders straight, boots heavy in the stillness.

The moment dissolved behind him.

But the weight of it didn't.

Locke turned from the confrontation, walking back across the grass toward the field tent. His boots crushed the scrub underfoot, each step louder than it needed to be.

From a distance, he could already tell—Amy wasn't watching the Julpa or the Vaylen family. Her posture was taut, angled toward the road stretching away from Pazuzu, eyes narrowed, mouth still.

As he got closer, she didn't move—just held his rifle out automatically, eyes never leaving whatever had caught her attention.

Locke took it without thinking. "What is it?"

Amy stood where he'd left her, jaw working a piece of gum. But she wasn't looking at him.

She was looking down the road.

"Something's coming," she murmured.

Locke frowned. "What?"

She didn't answer. Just stared—focused, squinting toward the far end of the carriageway where the stalled traffic thinned into distance and haze.

Locke turned.

There was movement. Not in the convoy—but through it.

Way down the stretch of road leading into the city, people were stepping aside. Slowly. Cautiously. One by one, like a silent wave rolling through the line of vehicles. Not panicked—just... unnerved. The way you move when something doesn't feel quite right.

A car door slammed. A child was pulled back behind a parent. Another stepped out of a vehicle just to stare.

The Julpa—the same one who, moments ago, had been ready to throw fists at a child and then Locke—was heading back to his car, clearly done with the previous interaction...then he froze.

His whole frame stiffened. Shoulders squared. Head tilted slightly—like he'd sensed something before he saw it.

The Vaylen father, crouched to retrieve the ball, halted mid-motion. His fingers brushed the grass but didn't close. His son stood beside him, utterly still, both of them staring silently down the same stretch of road.

The air changed. A drop in temperature. A shift in pressure. That old, primal sensation before the sky splits open with rain followed by a crack of thunder.

The Julpa turned fully now. Not in retreat—but recognition. Something deeper than fear.

Locke's eyes snapped back down the road.

Through the exhaust haze and dipping sun, a figure emerged—not running, not gliding, but moving with the kind of unnatural calm that unsettled everything it passed. Each step unhurried, every motion precise. No hesitation. Unaware of the disruption it was causing.

It walked the white line between the lanes. Straight, steady. People stepped aside instinctively, without being told.

The closer it came, the quieter everything around it seemed to fall—like the sound itself was stepping out of the way.

Then, it passed through the last row of cars, sunlight flaring behind it—and Locke saw the silhouette fully.

His breath caught.

Tall. Still. Human in form—nothing alien or monstrous about it. Just... wrong in all the ways that mattered.

Its eyes were fixed dead ahead. No fear. No uncertainty. No choice.

An Aetherien.

Drawn by whatever shift had already begun.

Heading straight for the gate.

Locke had first learned about the Aetheriens in school—buried somewhere between the Ash Dawn and the formation of the NetherKind Cities. Even then, they hadn't been framed as a threat. More like a phenomenon. An omen.

Every recorded instance in history described a lone Aetherien. Always solitary. Always singular. They didn't fight. They didn't speak. They simply appeared—drawn to the brink of change. Death. Disaster. Revelation and revolution.

Glimpsed on the edge of moments—standing at the site of a tragedy seconds before it happened, or walking alone through a town that would, days later, be lost to fire or flood.

But not all turning points were grim. Aetheriens had been witnessed observing peace summits that brought centuries of conflict to an end. At the founding of cities that would go on to become sanctuaries. At births, coronations, and great migrations—moments when the world seemed to pause, exhale, and quietly shift course for the better.

They didn't belong to any city. They held no allegiance. But their presence was never meaningless. They could walk among people without being noticed at all but when they wanted to be seen, when they allowed it—everyone felt it.

Some said they were harbingers of death, ushering the recently departed onto the next plane. Others believed they came to encourage, to bear witness to acts of defiance or rebirth. No one knew for sure. Only that their presence always meant one thing: Something was about to change.

The last widely reported appearance was in 1945, just outside what is now known as New Hinode, the NetherKind city in Japan. An Aetherien arrived hours before the bombing that nearly wiped out the entire NetherKind and human population in the area. This was the first time in decades that an Aetherien had been sighted.

And right now one was heading straight for Pazuzu.

Locke snapped his hand to the shoulder mic. "Eyes up. Are you seeing this?"

The response came through static—Jones, sounding rattled. "Yeah... yeah, we see it. What the hell is that?"

Before Locke could answer, the long-range radio at his side crackled to life.

"This is South Gate. We have a situation. Over."

Locke grabbed it, heart already hammering. "This is North. Go ahead, South."

A beat. Then: "We've got...we've got an Aetherien. Sir—it's right in front of the gate."

Locke froze. "West Gate, report."

A tense pause.

"...Same here. Aetherien. Just... standing there."

"Shit," Locke muttered under his breath.

He was already moving—half-run, half-sprint—back toward the gate road. "East, do you copy?"

"Copy. We see one approaching. Not at the gate yet, but it's coming."

Four gates. Four Aetheriens.

He stopped short, forcing calm into his voice. "Do not engage. Repeat—do not engage. No weapons raised. Eyes on, fingers off triggers."

The Aetherien approaching the North Gate had slowed to a stop, now standing just metres from where Locke had sprinted to position.

He froze, eyes locked on the figure—tall, unmoving, and framed by the flicker of the fading light of the day. They stood so close now that Locke could see the faint shimmer dancing across its skin—subtle at first, but unmistakable. The glow wasn't radiant. It was clinical. Cold.

Locke found himself staring. Not out of awe—he couldn't help it. The figure towered, not just in stature but in presence. And yet… it didn't look at him. Didn't even seem to notice him. Its gaze remained fixed, vacant, aimed somewhere far beyond him—straight down the road, toward the heart of Pazuzu City.

Behind the Aetherien, a crowd had begun to form. People from the stranded cars had drifted forward in slow, hesitant waves, drawn by curiosity, confusion… or something deeper, keeping their distance, forming a loose half-circle across the road. Faces—some pale with fear, others wide-eyed with wonder. One man held his phone aloft, filming shakily. A kid whispered something to their father and was immediately hushed. It wasn't chaos. It wasn't panic. It was reverence wrapped in tension. Like a crowd gathering at the edge of an eclipse.

A voice behind Locke, low and uneasy: "It's just standing there…"

Another answered, barely above a whisper. "Feels like it's looking right through us."

"Think it even knows we're here?" someone else asked—tone caught between curiosity and dread.

No reply. Just the quiet scrape of boots adjusting position. Fingers tightened on rifles. Still no one raised them.

The Aetherien didn't flinch. Didn't blink. Its expression didn't shift. It didn't scan its surroundings or react to the dozens of soldiers now lining up behind Locke with weapons lowered but ready. It simply... stood. Like it had been carved from stillness.

Four had appeared. One outside each of Pazuzu's gates. And the world had responded with silence.

Locke tried to read the Aetherien's face, searching for some glimmer of intent, but there was nothing. No recognition. No reaction. It was like trying to connect with a statue.

Whatever it was, whatever had brought it here, Locke wasn't part of it. He was a bystander. And the Aetherien's disregard made that painfully clear. He could've waved a hand in its face and it likely wouldn't have noticed. Or cared.

The chill in his stomach settled deeper.

Locke could feel the tension ripple down the line behind him, his soldiers watching, waiting. No one dared move. The stillness wasn't just visual—it had weight. Presence.

And Locke—despite the uniform, the command, the training—felt helpless. Small.

They were either about to witness history… or watch the world come apart at the seams.

He couldn't shake the feeling it would be the latter.

EPILOGUE

猫の三姉妹

(The Neko No Sanshimai)

Tick. Tick.

It was just past 1 a.m. in New Hinode—Japan's sleepless jewel and the most modern of the NetherKind Cities. Above the electric sprawl of the entertainment district, neon kanji shimmered against steel and glass, bathing the alleyways below in fractured colour. Among it all, tucked quietly between a 24-hour bookshop and a shuttered teahouse, one building refused to compete for attention.

The Three Cat Sisters' sushi restaurant breathed with a still, measured pulse—its presence marked not by noise or brightness, but by calm.

Mounted above the entrance, a slab of polished black granite offered no invitation. No name. No lights. No branding. Just three cat silhouettes, identical and exact, carved clean through the stone. Sleek. Upright. Unmoving.

A single spotlight shone down on the sign from above—subtle, deliberate—casting the hollowed cat figures onto the ground below. Their shadows stretched long across the pavement like sentries at attention, watching the street in silence.

Tick. Tick.

Every high table was taken, but the room never felt crowded. The soft clink of ceramic and the low murmur of conversation wove seamlessly into the slow, hypnotic rhythm of the sushi train. Plates drifted past in a continuous loop—

delicate maki, translucent sashimi, lacquered eel—each arranged with quiet precision by unseen hands.

No one hurried. Even at this hour, there was no sense of lateness—only stillness. This was the kind of place where time loosened its grip, where the weight of the city melted quietly at the threshold.

Those who came here understood this wasn't just a restaurant. It was a sanctuary.

The diners were left to their peace. Some spoke in hushed tones, their words softened by the space around them. Others ate in silence, grateful for the solitude. There was no pressure to perform politeness. No obligation to smile or make small talk. Just stillness, and the slow, steady rhythm of a place that asked nothing in return.

Tick. Tick.

The interior was low-lit and cocooned in warmth, its shadows gentle and deliberate. Light pooled softly from paper-shaded lanterns overhead, casting a golden hush across the polished wood and woven mats. The edges of the room faded into a comfortable darkness—never oppressive, just out of reach.

Along the far wall, a water feature stretched the full length of the room. Sheets of clear water flowed down angled black stone in an unbroken stream, whispering rather than splashing. It fell into a still basin below with no flourish, no demand to be noticed—more a heartbeat than a decoration. Alive in its own quiet way.

Set into the surrounding walls, gentle alcoves curved inward like resting breath. Within each, a modest arrangement of greenery—ferns, mosses, slow-reaching vines—offered life without decoration.

Near the rear of the room, one alcove held something more.

Nestled among the foliage sat a small porcelain Maneki-neko. Its painted paw rose and fell in a slow, mechanical rhythm—steady, unfaltering, eternal.

Tick. Tick.

Most customers didn't notice it at first. But those who came back, those who stayed long enough to see beneath the surface, always did. It watched without watching. Present, but never demanding attention.

Always waving.

The Elder Sister moved silently through the room, unseen until she was needed. She refilled tea, replaced sake, cleared dishes with effortless grace. She never hovered. Never interrupted. Her presence was like the air—only noticed in its absence. One moment she was there, the next, gone.

New Hinode had been built from ash.

When the old city fell in the mid-twentieth century, its survivors stood at a crossroads: grieve what had been lost, or shape something new from the wreckage. They chose to rebuild—not as a replica, but as a response. What rose wasn't a monument to what had been, but a challenge to what might come next. Sharper. Louder. Resilient.

Tradition wasn't discarded. It was reformed—threaded through steel and circuitry, running parallel to change, not behind it.

Tick. Tick.

The Three Cat Sisters were no exception.

In the days of Old Hinode—before war and fire reshaped the city—they had worked quietly in the margins, tucked into alleyways and temples, their purpose hidden. Now, in New Hinode, they stood exactly where they always had—only now behind a counter, blades in hand, beneath the glow of paper lanterns and hollow-eyed cat statues.

The city had changed. The duty had not.

On the surface, it was a place of comfort. Of tradition. Of exceptional food prepared with care and served with quiet grace. But beneath the warmth and routine, the restaurant served its true purpose—a carefully held front for the work the Sisters had carried out for centuries.

They were protectors. Guardians of balance. Not just of place, but of order.

Their duty was to the natural world—not in reverence, but in defence. Against what didn't belong. Against forces that twisted the boundaries of life, and sometimes, against people who did the same.

That was why they existed. Why they were created.

Born into an age when Japan's provinces were fractured by war, the Sisters had never answered to lords or emperors. They were not agents of conquest. They had no allegiance to power. Their work was older than politics. Older than cities.

Their role was balance. And balance didn't fade just because the world had changed.

There had always been three. That was the way it had always been.

When one stepped down—through age, through injury, or through death—another rose to take her place. A sister. A daughter. A cousin. Always blood. Not for sentiment. Not for tradition. But because it had to be.

Their strength wasn't just in training or discipline. It was in trust. Instinctive. Unspoken and bone deep.

Each new Sister was chosen from within, shaped by those who came before her. She inherited more than a role—she inherited a rhythm, a purpose, a weight that stretched back through centuries. That was how the line endured: through continuity. Through memory. Through quiet, unwavering resolve.

Above them sat the Mother, Sanshimi. Not appointed nor crowned but earned.

She had once been one of them. Now, she was their anchor—their stillness in the current. She rarely spoke, but when she did, her words landed like a stone dropped in water. No motion wasted or without purpose.

It was said that when something stirred—something unnatural, something wrong—it was Sanshimi who felt it first.

And by the time she did, the Sisters were already moving.

Tick. Tick.

The conveyor belt moved with a steady, unchanging rhythm—calm, deliberate, almost hypnotic. The Maneki-neko watched over the restaurant. Its painted eyes, wide and unblinking, seemed to track the room with quiet vigilance. The arm bobbed in its familiar mechanical arc—up, down, up again—like a heartbeat the space had learned to breathe with.

Two of the Three Sisters worked behind the counter with quiet precision, slicing, rolling, and arranging sushi with an elegance that came from blood rather than years. The youngest—just fourteen—moved with focused care, her motions deliberate, each cut made with the kind of discipline others might mistake for caution. She didn't speak, didn't hesitate, and rarely looked up.

Beside her, the middle sister—twenty-three—was faster, more fluid. There was a quiet confidence in the way she moved, her hands a blur as she assembled each plate with practiced ease. Her posture was relaxed, but sharp. Always aware.

Together, they formed a rhythm of their own—youth and experience balanced in motion.

The third Sister—the eldest—moved through the dining area. She was the face the customers saw—the one who met their eyes, listened, and made them feel like they belonged. Her movements were unhurried, but purposeful. She topped up tea, offered quiet acknowledgements, and slipped away before small talk could disturb the room's calm.

Her role wasn't lesser. It was intentional. She carried the weight of presence. Of protection.

The Maneki-neko's arm bobbed.

Tick. Tick.

A soft, mechanical rhythm that had echoed through Sanshimi's life—through her mother's, and her mother's mother's. A quiet legacy. A bloodline of protectors.

Tick. Tick. Tick...

The rhythm softened.

Not by volume, but by presence—its constancy thinning, like breath stretched too far between beats.

Tick...

Tick...

And then—nothing.

At first, no one noticed. The motion that had quietly punctuated the restaurant for as long as anyone could remember had simply... stopped. One customer, seated alone near the far end of the conveyor belt, paused mid-bite. He frowned slightly, chopsticks hovering in place as he stared at the still figure of the waving cat. A few seats down, another patron looked up. Her brow furrowed. She glanced toward the Maneki-neko, then toward the staff, sensing something unspoken in the air. A ripple moved through the room—small glances, uncertain pauses, utensils placed more gently than before. Conversations faltered. Postures stiffened. The atmosphere hadn't broken. It had tightened. The absence of motion sat heavy in the space where sound had once lived. Drawn in like breath held too long, waiting for something to move.

A third customer caught on. Then a fourth.

Silence spread—not sudden, but inevitable. Like water soaking into fabric, it crept between conversations, muffling words mid-sentence. Within seconds, the vibrant hum that had warmed the room dissolved into stillness.

Behind the counter, the Sisters stopped. Blades hovered mid-motion, the final slices suspended in air before being set down with quiet care—each movement deliberate, each gesture weighted.

The third Sister—the one who moved among the guests—turned without a word and crossed the floor. Her steps were unhurried, precise, as she approached a narrow panel hidden in the wall near the entrance. She opened it with a practiced hand and flicked a single switch.

The conveyor belt slowed. Its motor exhaled a fading whir, then wound down to nothing. Plates trembled slightly as the movement ceased, settling in place as if they too had sensed the shift—bracing for whatever came next.

No one asked what was happening. They didn't need to.

The understanding moved between them—not in words, but in the low, ancient murmur of instinct. Without prompting, they gathered their belongings. Chairs were pushed in softly. Money was left on the tables with quiet precision. Not as payment. As respect.

Some bowed their heads slightly as they passed the Sisters. Others simply left in silence, stepping out into the New Hinode night without looking back.

The last customer paused briefly at the door. He turned to glance once more at the cat—frozen, still—then stepped through and was gone, swallowed by the glow of the city beyond.

Tinow, the middle sister, crossed the floor and turned the lock with a soft click.

The restaurant was empty now. Empty, save for the Three Cat Sisters. And Sanshimi.

No one spoke. No one moved.

The stillness of the cat echoed through the room, its paw suspended mid-wave, unmoving. The soft fall of water from the wall-length feature was the only sound that remained—gentle, fluid, unbothered by the weight pressing in around it.

They had all heard it.

Not a sound exactly, but a call—subtle, unmistakable. Felt more than heard.

Something unnatural had stirred.

Something had broken loose.

Not a ghost. Not a spirit.

Not the usual creeping sickness that sometimes bled through the cracks in the natural world.

No.

This was different.

Older.

Ancient.

The Sisters waited. Their posture remained calm, but not at ease.

They did not reach for weapons. They did not speak. They simply stood—still, listening—as if attuned to something just outside the range of human hearing.

At the centre of the restaurant, beneath the now motionless Maneki-neko, Sanshimi stood with her head tilted upward.

Her eyes met the cat's unblinking stare.

She didn't move.

She didn't blink.

When she spoke, her voice came low. Measured.

"彼女が剣を持っている."

She has the sword.

END OF PART ONE

Thank you for reading

ECHOES OF ASH PART ONE - BLOOD & VINYL

This is only the beginning.

Part One was released early to give readers a first look at the world of Heidi Evervale—a chance to discover the tone, the stakes, and the characters before the full journey unfolds.

The complete story will span six parts, each one expanding the world, raising the tension, and revealing the truth behind Heidi, the situation she finds herself in, and the forces that shaped them both.

If you've enjoyed the story so far, you can follow the journey online and help support the book as it grows.

Every share, comment, or review helps bring more readers into the world—and every reader helps keep it alive.

PART TWO COMING SOON!

APPENDIX 1: Excerpts from History

The World of Echoes of Ash

Exploring the World and Characters Beyond the Story The Archives are more than a collection of historical records, newspaper clippings, and personal memoirs—they are a gateway to a world far larger than Heidi Evervale's story. They unravel the intricate societies, shifting cultures, and defining events that shaped both past and present, breathing life into the world she inhabits. From pivotal moments in history to deeply personal reflections, The Archives chronicle triumphs, tragedies, and untold secrets, revealing the forces that have sculpted this ever-evolving landscape.

Beyond simply expanding the lore of Heidi: Echoes of Ash, The Archives weave a rich, intricate backdrop that reveals how this world has transformed over time, leading to the moment we first step into the novel. They introduce characters, events, and hidden histories—some whispering at the edges of Heidi's journey, others standing apart yet holding subtle significance. Even where something appears distant or entirely unrelated to Heidi's story, there is no coincidence in its inclusion; every thread, no matter how small, is woven into the larger narrative and is sure to have implications yet to unfold.

But this is only the beginning. The Archives will continue to grow, expanding with new discoveries, untold histories, and unseen connections that shape the world beyond what we know. This is just the first step into a much larger world—one whose history is still being uncovered.

APPENDIX 1.1

> Field Notes of the First Vampire Colony
>
> *A Chronicle by Alberto Grace (1218)*

This account is not written as a tale of legend or fantasy, nor is it an attempt to romanticise the unknown. It is a simple documentation of what I have witnessed and learned—a record of a civilisation that exists in the shadows, unseen by human eyes, yet older than any empire that has ever risen or fallen.

The journey that led me to the heart of the vampire colony in the remote territories of the east has proven to be an unparalleled discovery, one that, should its truth ever reach the ears of men, could shift the course of history itself. What I encountered was not a savage horde of bloodthirsty creatures, nor a cabal of scheming predators lurking beneath human society. Instead, I found a people—structured, disciplined, and bound by traditions that predate even our earliest recorded histories.

The vampires live under a self-imposed veil of isolation, not out of fear, but out of choice. They have no desire to be known. No need for conquest. Their ways are complex, their endurance legendary, and their restraint a testament to their mastery over the very nature that defines them.

The Hidden City

The colony lies far beyond the reach of human settlements, buried deep within the ancient forests where even the most seasoned hunters dare not tread. To the untrained eye, there is nothing but tangled undergrowth and impassable terrain, but to those who know where to look, the entrance is hidden within a vast network of caverns, swallowed by time and the slow creep of moss and stone. It is a place where the seasons do not touch, where the cold of the outside world gives way to an underground heat, sustained by natural hot springs that run beneath the colony itself.

Though hidden, it is not primitive. Its architecture is deliberate, precise—too refined to be the work of mere erosion. Vast halls have been shaped by unseen hands, their pillars marked with symbols I do not recognise. The tunnels are wide and interconnected, forming what can only be described as a city of silence, where time itself seems to move at a slower pace.

It is not a place built for war, yet neither is it a sanctuary in the traditional sense. It is something beyond that—a monument to survival.

The Vampires Themselves

The vampires resemble humans, but there is a refinement to their form that sets them apart. Their skin, though pale, is not unnatural; rather, it carries the hue of someone who has never known the warmth of the sun. Their eyes, dark yet luminous, shift subtly when they are stirred by emotion, though they do not betray their thoughts easily. Their movements are precise, controlled—lacking any wasted effort, yet never mechanical.

There is a quiet strength in their presence, but also an unsettling stillness. It is as though they have perfected the art of economy in all things—never hurried, never restless, never indulgent in excess motion or speech.

I did not witness any signs of age among them. Whether this is due to the slowed aging process often speculated upon in myths, or something more profound, I do not know. But it is clear that these beings do not experience time as we do.

The Ritual of Feeding

Perhaps the most startling revelation was their method of sustenance. Contrary to human fears, they do not hunt indiscriminately, nor do they require the blood of men to survive. Instead, the colony maintains livestock, raising them with a care and patience that borders on reverence.

Cattle, goats, and sheep are bred with meticulous attention to their health, their diets carefully regulated. The vampires feed in a manner that is neither savage nor excessive, taking only what is needed and ensuring that the animals recover. It is a practice far removed from the grotesque legends told in human villages, yet its very efficiency is what makes it unsettling—a reminder that they have perfected the art of survival in ways that we have only begun to understand.

A Society of Order

The colony is governed by an entity known as the Head of the House, though the title is not inherited. Unlike human monarchies, their leadership is determined by wisdom and time—earned, not given. The Head is both ruler and guide, a position of great weight but not absolute authority.

Beneath them, the society is divided into smaller factions, each responsible for different aspects of their way of life—governance, preservation, and observation of the outside world. Their decisions are not made lightly, nor are they made quickly. To a human, their deliberations would seem painfully slow, yet to the vampires, patience is a foundation of strength.

They do not marry in the human sense, but they form bonds—partnerships that last centuries, forged through mutual respect rather than fleeting passion. These bonds are not broken lightly, nor are they formed impulsively.

The Offer of Eternity

When my time among them neared its end, I was summoned by the Head of the House.

"You have witnessed the ways of our kind," he said. "You have seen how we live. Yet there is more we can offer you."

What followed was an invitation—not a demand, nor a threat. A proposal, rare and deliberate, extended only to those they deemed worthy. I was given the choice to join them, to step beyond the limits of mortality and into their world.

I declined. Not out of fear, but out of duty.

Even as I turned away, I knew I would never see them again.

A Final Warning

Before I left, the Head of the House left me with words that have haunted me ever since.

"You wonder why we do not rise up and conquer," he said. "We are already the dominant species, but we choose not to act on it. We do not need to conquer; we simply exist. And in that, we are superior."

It was not a boast. It was not a threat. It was a truth spoken with indifference, as though he had seen human civilisations rise and fall so many times that the very notion of dominance had lost its meaning.

They had the power. But they had no desire to prove it.

Conclusion

I leave this place with more questions than I arrived with. The vampires I encountered are not the creatures of nightmares, nor the villains of our myths. They are a people—older than our greatest cities, wiser than our longest dynasties, and stronger than any force that has ever sought to erase them.

They have mastered restraint, but in that restraint lies something more terrifying than any war machine: patience.

One day, they may choose to step out of the shadows. And when they do, it will not be with fire and conquest. It will be with the quiet, absolute certainty of something that was never meant to be beneath us.

If that day ever comes, we will not be ready.

APPENDIX 1.2

> ## MAVIS DEACON & THE RENEGADES
>
> *A Retrospective Look at the Bands Rise and Fall*

Legends Lost: The Rise and Fall of Mavis Deacon & The Renegades

It's impossible to talk about the glory days of 90s rock without mentioning Mavis Deacon & The Renegades. With two groundbreaking albums that defined an era and sold-out world tours, the band seemed destined for immortality. At the heart of their success was the creative duo of Mavis Deacon, the fiery frontwoman, and Ellis Evervale, the drummer whose beats and lyrics perfectly complemented her raw energy.

Mavis and Ellis first met as teenagers in secondary school in Manchester, where they both grew up. Bonding over their shared love of music, they began collaborating almost immediately, forming the foundation of a creative partnership that would later captivate millions. By the time Mavis Deacon & The Renegades played their first gig in 1994, they had already built a reputation for their raw energy and tight chemistry on stage.

Their debut album, released in 1998, was a global phenomenon, introducing the world to Mavis's searing vocals and Ellis's driving rhythms. Critics hailed it as the voice of a generation, and it quickly climbed the charts. But it was their second album, released in 2000, that cemented their place in rock history. A perfect storm of heartfelt lyrics, unforgettable melodies, and explosive performances, it shattered expectations, going multi-platinum and dominating airwaves worldwide. The band toured relentlessly, playing to sold-out arenas and earning a devoted fanbase that hung on every note.

But in 2001, their meteoric rise came to a halt when Ellis abruptly left the band, shaking its foundation and reshaping its legacy forever.

Ellis Speaks: "There Was Never a Choice"

Ellis Evervale sat down with us to discuss his time with the band under one condition: no questions about his niece, Heidi, beyond the circumstances surrounding his departure.

"I loved that band more than anything in the world," Ellis said. "Leaving wasn't a choice. It wasn't artistic differences. It was life. I had this new responsibility—raising my niece after my sister died—and it wasn't about me anymore. I had to take care of someone who depended on me completely. Imagine that. It was hard enough looking after myself, let alone a baby."

When asked about the early days, Ellis's tone softened.

"Those first two albums… they were magic, weren't they?" he said, a small smile creeping onto his face.

"I remember late nights in the studio, me and Mavis bouncing ideas off each other, arguing over lyrics, laughing when we finally got it right. There was this energy—like the music was pulling itself out of us. I've never felt anything like it since."

He paused, his expression shifting as he remembered their performances on stage. "And then, when we got out there... God, the way she held that stage. It wasn't just her voice—it was everything about her. She could command an entire room with one look, one note. I'd be behind the kit, watching the crowd lose their minds, and it wasn't just about the music. It was her. She was magnetic. She still is."

Ellis gave a small, almost wistful laugh. "Mavis was never just good—she was something else entirely. The best I've ever worked with, no question."

Mavis on the Split: "Those Songs Were Knives" - The band continued without Ellis, but cracks began to show over time. In 2010, Mavis made a controversial decision that would alter the band's trajectory forever. On the cusp of touring for their sixth album, the band announced they would no longer be performing songs from their first two albums. The backlash was immediate and intense, alienating a loyal fanbase who had built their connection to the band through those iconic early hits.

When asked about the decision, Mavis reflected with a mix of defiance and vulnerability.

"That... that was a moment, right?" she began. "You see, here's the thing. And any member of any band will tell you this. You sing and play the same songs each and every night. And each and every night, you give it your all. No matter what. No matter what's going on in your life, when you're on that stage, you're on that stage for the people who've travelled to see you. They've devoted their time to come and sing, to bare their soul in a space where they can leave behind every shitty thing going on in their lives, just for one evening. That's the breath some people need to keep going." She continued, more assured now. "But here's the other thing. For me, there was no escape. Offstage, onstage, in the studio, writing... singing those fucking songs every night. The songs I wrote and performed with Ellis—but he wasn't there anymore. Each song from those first two albums… singing each one was like a knife being driven into my chest. That's why I did what I did. I wasn't being petulant. I just couldn't do it anymore."

Despite the pain, Mavis smiled when she talked about the early days.

"The first two albums… we were kids, weren't we? Kids with something to prove. I remember Ellis—he'd come up with these ideas that were just… out of nowhere.

Sometimes it was a drumbeat, sometimes it was a lyric, sometimes a melody. And it wasn't just one moment, either. He'd do it all the time. You'd be sitting there, frustrated because nothing was clicking, and then bam—he'd say something, or tap out a rhythm, and suddenly we'd have a song. It felt effortless, even though it wasn't."

She leaned back slightly, lost in thought. "Those late nights in the studio, bouncing ideas back and forth… God, the arguments we had over the tiniest things. But it always worked. I don't know how to explain it, but we just… clicked. The way his ideas fit with mine, it was like they were meant to. That's what made those albums what they were. There was this magic in the process, and I haven't felt that with anyone else since."

By the time their fourth album was released, Mavis had already started writing songs for other artists to perform. "I needed a new outlet," she explained. "I'd lost my passion for The Renegades, but I hadn't lost my love for writing. So, I wrote for others. Some of those tracks ended up being bigger hits than anything we ever did with the band."

The Pit: Ellis's Legacy - Meanwhile, Ellis channeled his passion for music into a different kind of project: The Pit, a live music venue he opened in 2004 with his best friend, Mijo.

"The Pit was always the dream," Ellis explained. "Even when I was with the band, I wanted a place where live music could thrive. It's not about fame or fortune. It's about the music, the connection, and giving people a stage."

The Pit quickly became a cornerstone of Pazuzu City's music scene, hosting both up-and-coming talent and surprise appearances by music legends. For Ellis, it's more than a venue—it's a legacy built on his love of music and the community it creates.

As our conversation came to a close, I asked Ellis the question that had lingered throughout the interview: Did he miss it all? "Of course," he said without hesitation. "But I'm in a great place now, and I wouldn't have what I have if I'd stayed. Again, there was no choice."

Fans and critics still debate what Mavis Deacon & The Renegades might have achieved if Ellis had stayed. Would the third album have been their greatest work? Could the band have risen to global superstardom? Or would the pressures of success have torn them apart regardless?

For Mavis and Ellis, the memories of those early years remain bittersweet. Their respect for each other is undeniable, even if reconciliation seems out of reach. Despite their ups and downs, the music they created together endures—a testament to a partnership that, for a time, defined an era.

Mavis Deacon & The Renegades may not have achieved all they could have, but their legacy lives on through the songs that once captured the hearts of millions.

APPENDIX 1.3

The Ghosts: Diary of Captain Norman Grey

Disclaimer from the Author: The Heidi mentioned in this account is not the Heidi Evervale of Heidi: Echoes of Ash. This Heidi was her human great-grandmother on her mother's side and the grandmother of Ellis and Nina Evervale.

21st May 1940

We are ghosts now. Left behind, forgotten, but not defeated. When the regiment fell back, we were cut off—a mix of humans and NetherKind stranded in this forsaken French countryside. Command must think we're dead already, lost to the chaos. Maybe they're right. But if death is to come for us, it won't find us cowering. It will find us fighting.

The others look to me as their leader, though God knows why. I am not the man for this. I am young, younger than many officers I have served under. They carried themselves with hardened eyes and steady hands, while I still feel the weight of every decision pressing on me. My hands betray me when I unholster my pistol, trembling just enough to remind me of my inexperience. Leadership feels heavier than my rifle today, especially when staring down such an unlikely company.

There are seven of us to start: myself, three other humans, and three NetherKind. The humans are Private Milligan, a medic with a sharp tongue and a sharper wit; Corporal Evans, a crack shot who rarely speaks; and Sergeant Harris, a scout with a talent for slipping through shadows. The NetherKind include Kaelar, a towering Julpa, his presence alone enough to make men hesitate; Dakkar, a Nyssari, who moves with unsettling silence; and Lira, a Vaylen, whose glowing markings shift like ripples in still water.

I had seen Lira before, back in the city. Not here. Not like this. Then, she had been surrounded by her own people, laughing, vibrant, her bioluminescent markings dancing across her skin. Now, she barely spoke, her glow dimmed to a hushed flicker. That's when I realised—the others who had been with her, the ones who made her glow so brightly, were not here. Which meant they were dead.

One of them, Kaelar, offered me water when my flask ran dry. His voice was a low rumble, his words soft despite his size. The gesture unnerved me more than it should have. Are they so different from us? Do they mourn? Do they fear death as we do? I'm not sure I want to know the answers.

We've made a pact: If we are to fall, it will not be without purpose. We've tracked a German regiment preparing to ambush our forces. If they succeed, hundreds will die. That is not a future I'll allow, not while we still have breath and bullets.

22nd May 1940: The Barn

The barn where we've made camp smells of damp hay and desperation. The walls whisper the stories of those who hid here before us, fleeing the same invaders we now face. A family's belongings are scattered in the corner—a child's toy, a woman's scarf. They've long since gone, leaving behind only ghosts. Perhaps they know we're here now. Perhaps they watch and hope.

Today, we welcomed new faces into our strange little regiment. A young woman emerged from the shadows of a nearby village, trembling but defiant. She's German by birth but an enemy of the Reich.

Her name is Heidi. She admitted to shooting a Nazi officer who was beating an elderly man in the square. She stood firm as she spoke, her voice steady, but her eyes burned with something unrelenting.

"We had to run," Heidi said.

The others were wary at first. A German among us? But war makes strange alliances. If we can stand beside demons, why not her? She has agreed to fight with us. I see no other choice. The fight ahead will require every hand, every ounce of courage we can muster.

23rd May 1940

We moved again today, putting more distance between ourselves and the enemy. The silence in the group is heavy. Every step feels like a march toward something none of us are ready for. Harris insists we're close to the regiment's supply wagons now. He's been ahead of us, scouting, his sharp eyes catching every detail. He looks at me when he reports back, waiting for my orders. I give them, but it doesn't feel like they're mine. They're just words that came from somewhere deep, somewhere that knows failure isn't an option.

Milligan tried to lighten the mood. He's a natural at it, throwing in a joke about our ragtag group being "the most dangerous circus in France." Kaelar chuckled, a deep rumble that seemed to break the tension for a moment. Even Evans cracked a smile.

I'm grateful for Milligan. I'm not good at lifting spirits. My mind is too full of what lies ahead, of the decisions that will likely lead some of these men and women to their deaths. It's hard to shake that thought.

24th May 1940

I used to think the NetherKind were monsters. They were stories told to keep us afraid of the dark, and later, the propaganda made them easy scapegoats for everything that went wrong in the world. Even now, I catch myself watching them too closely, as if they might turn on us at any moment.

But today, as we followed the German regiment, I saw something else. Kaelar took first watch last night. When I woke to relieve him, he had quietly tended the fire, ensuring it stayed warm enough to keep us from freezing but dim enough not to give us away. Dakkar caught a hare for breakfast without a word, sharing it with Harris before anyone else. And Lira, when Milligan was fumbling to fix a strap on his pack, simply walked over and adjusted it for him. No fanfare, no words, just a silent gesture.

These aren't the monsters I was warned about. They're people—different, yes, but people. If others could see what

I've seen, they might think differently too. Perhaps this war has given us more than just loss. Perhaps it's shown us that we are stronger together.

24th May 1940 (continued)

We've kept to the shadows, following the German regiment's trail. They march like a machine, relentless and unyielding. But machines have weaknesses. They grow overconfident, blind to what lurks beyond their ordered lines.

The closer we get, the more cracks we see in their formation. Their supply wagons are under-guarded, their officers too confident in the safety of these back roads. It's clear they aren't expecting trouble, and that will be their downfall.

Tonight, Kaelar made a flippant remark that stuck with me. "We're just ghosts trailing their steps, Captain," he said, his gravelly voice carrying a hint of humour. Ghosts. The name feels fitting. We're invisible to them, haunting their every move, waiting to strike. Perhaps we are ghosts, in a way—lost to our own world, yet still fighting for it.

As we rested by a shallow stream, I asked each of the Ghosts to write letters to their loved ones. If we do not survive, someone must carry their words home. It's a grim task, but a necessary one. Heidi's letter caught my eye as she folded it. Her handwriting is bold and sharp, much like the woman herself.

I wrote my own letter to Elizabeth. I told her of the stars tonight, how they look brighter here than I've ever seen. I told her not to weep if the letter finds her. Let it remind her that I stood for something when it mattered most.

26th May 1940: The Night Before the Battle

The attack is set for dawn. We spent the night preparing, each of us playing a part in the plan. Harris scouted ahead, mapping the regiment's route and marking their weakest points. Evans checked our weapons, ensuring every rifle and grenade was ready. Milligan packed supplies, muttering under his breath about the futility of it all. The NetherKind prepared in their own ways.

Milligan, ever the restless one, pulled out a bottle he had tucked away in his pack. "No sense in dying sober," he muttered, taking a swig before passing it on. One by one, we drank—Harris, Evans, even Dakkar, who wrinkled his nose at the burn but didn't refuse.

Lira barely sipped, but she lingered as she passed it back, her bioluminescent markings pulsing faintly in the firelight. "For remembrance," she murmured, the glow fading to something sombre.

Before the fire died, Heidi spoke up. "If we're ghosts," she said, "then let's haunt them properly." The others laughed, but there was steel in her voice. For a moment, I forgot she was new to this fight. She's one of us now.

26th May 1940: The Attack

The morning came too soon. We moved before first light, slipping through the trees, our footfalls swallowed by the damp earth. The German regiment was still at rest, their sentries lazy, unaware of the storm creeping toward them.

Harris and Evans took position first, rifles steady. Dakkar vanished into the mist, his Nyssari instincts making him a phantom among the trees. Lira, ever calculating, mapped out angles, whispering low to Milligan about potential fallback points—not that we expected to use them.

Then Kaelar moved.

Like a rolling tide, he surged forward, silent and brutal. The first German soldier barely had time to register the Julpa's approach before Kaelar's axe cleaved through him. Chaos erupted. Gunfire. Shouting. The Germans scrambled, caught off guard.

Evans took down an officer before they could rally. Harris disappeared into the smoke, re-emerging seconds later with a knife buried in an enemy's side. Heidi, fearless as ever, fired shot after shot, reloading with sharp efficiency.

A German officer, alerted to Kaelar's presence after watching him cut through his men, raised his pistol and fired. The bullets embedded into Kaelar's thick hide, drawing grunts of pain but never breaking his momentum. He barely acknowledged them, swatting at his side like a man brushing away flies before plowing forward.

And then the tide turned.

They regrouped faster than we expected, their numbers overwhelming. A bullet caught Milligan in the side—he dropped, cursing, blood pooling beneath him. Dakkar took out three before one of them caught him in the back.

Lira fought with precision, her glowing patterns flickering through the mist like a phantom. I caught glimpses of her—a flash of movement, a shimmer of bioluminescence—but then she was gone, swallowed by the melee. When I saw her again, it was too late. Her glow had faded to nothing.

Kaelar fought like a beast of legend, his massive form carving a path toward their command. He reached them, tearing through their officers before they could issue another order. I saw the moment the Germans realised they had lost their leadership—the hesitation, the faltering steps. That was our opening.

Harris shouted for a retreat, but there were too few of us left to run. Evans fell next, a bullet through the throat. Milligan was still alive, barely, but we couldn't reach him. Heidi and I fired until our weapons clicked empty, then fought with knives, fists—anything.

Then Kaelar went down.

Even on his knees, he was a force to be reckoned with, crushing skulls, breaking bones. But there were too many. A dozen bayonets found him at once, piercing his massive frame. He roared, not in pain, but in defiance. Still, he fought. It took six—seven—German soldiers to bring him down. They swarmed him, ropes and bayonets pinning his arms, hands clawing at his throat.

I saw Heidi react before I could, grabbing a rifle from one of the fallen Nazi's, raising and firing. Three fell before she ran out of bullets. Then, with a snarl, she charged, knife in hand. She took three more before they knocked her to the ground.

Kaelar hit the earth a second later. Unmoving.

I don't remember when I hit the ground. There was shouting, movement, but it all blurred. The last thing I saw was Heidi, bloodied but standing, dragging Milligan toward cover.

The world faded.

28th May 1940

I woke to silence. The battle was won, but we had lost everything.

I counted the bodies. Harris. Evans. Dakkar. Lira. Kaelar.

Milligan was breathing, barely. Heidi sat beside him, staring at nothing.

"We did it," she whispered.

We did.

But at what cost?

29th June 1940

The battle for Dunkirk is over. Thousands have been saved, ferried across the channel to fight another day. Behind closed doors, Command acknowledged our efforts.

I now carry a handful of letters. Words of love, of regret, of promises never kept. I swore to deliver them if I made it out. Now, I must.

"You've done the impossible, Captain Norman Grey," they told me. I wanted to laugh. Impossible is what happens when desperation meets resolve. But I said nothing. This war is far from over, and our work has only begun.

They call us heroes, but we don't feel like heroes. We're still ghosts, shadows cast by a fire that will one day consume us. But if history remembers us, let it remember this:

We fought not for glory, but for each other. For the chance to see another dawn.

APPENDIX 1.4

The Birth of the First Known Half-Human, Half-Vampire Sparks Global Debate

By: Sabrina Hargrove, Senior Correspondent

Pazuzu City — In an unprecedented turn of events, a child of unimaginable origins has been born into the world: Heidi Everdale, the first known half-human, half-vampire. The revelation has sent shockwaves through both human and NetherKind communities, leaving experts, lawmakers, and citizens scrambling to understand the implications of such an existence.

Heidi's birth, initially kept under wraps, came to light only recently. Her mother, Nina Everdale, a human, tragically passed away shortly after giving birth. The identity of Heidi's father remains unknown, leading to significant speculation. One possibility being considered is that Nina was bitten during her pregnancy, though this theory has been widely dismissed given that vampire attacks have not been recorded for centuries. Vampires, known for their nomadic and reclusive nature, are believed unlikely to have been involved. Nevertheless, all avenues are being explored in this unprecedented case.

The child's guardian, Ellis Everdale, a former musician and drummer for the legendary rock band Mavis Deacon & The Renegades, fled to Pazuzu City, a prominent NetherKind metropolis in the UK, seeking refuge and protection. Pazuzu City, renowned for its policies favoring NetherKind rights, has become a focal point of the global debate.

Ellis has remained private about the circumstances surrounding Heidi's birth but was visibly emotional when questioned about the global controversy. According to caseworker Rose Calloway, who has taken on Ellis's case, he became visibly angry when reporters questioned Heidi's right to exist. "Ellis is doing his best in a situation no one could prepare for," Rose said on his behalf. "He's made it clear that Heidi is just a child. She didn't choose to be born, nor did she choose her nature. It's up to us to ensure she's not punished for circumstances beyond her control."

The revelation of Heidi's existence has sparked heated debates worldwide. On one side, skeptics fear what her existence might represent—a possible blurring of the boundaries between human and NetherKind. On the other, advocates like Calloway stress the importance of focusing on Heidi's individuality rather than her heritage.

"This is not just about a child with an unusual parentage," Calloway stated. "This is about whether we, as a society, are capable of seeing beyond our fears and prejudices. Every individual, human or NetherKind, deserves to be judged by their actions, not their birth. Heidi is innocent, and it's our duty to protect her from being vilified for simply existing."

The Pazuzu City Council, which has long served as a beacon of safety for NetherKind, has voiced its tentative support for Ellis and Heidi. However, officials are bracing for legal and political battles that may challenge the city's capacity to provide sanctuary.

Historian and NetherKind relations expert Dr. Miranda Holt commented on the broader implications. "The birth of Heidi Everdale challenges every preconceived notion we have about identity and coexistence," Holt said. "While many fear what she represents, her existence may also provide an opportunity to foster deeper understanding between humans and NetherKind. But the questions this raises—about genetics, societal boundaries, and integration—are not ones we can answer overnight."

Despite the overwhelming attention, Ellis's priority remains Heidi's safety. Calloway noted that Ellis's outburst of anger during questioning stemmed from a deep frustration with the relentless scrutiny surrounding Heidi. "Heidi is a child," Calloway said firmly. "She deserves the chance to grow up in peace, to be valued for who she is—not feared for what she is."

The growing controversy is not without its political ramifications. While Pazuzu City remains a safe haven, the incident has reignited tensions between human governments and NetherKind leadership worldwide. Some fear that the case will further polarize already fragile relations, while others see it as a chance to push for greater acceptance and understanding.

As the world watches, Heidi Everdale has become more than just a child—she is a symbol of change, fear, and possibility. Her future, and the world's response to her existence, will undoubtedly shape the course of history for both humans and NetherKind.

The question remains: Can society rise above its fears to embrace a new era of coexistence, or will Heidi's existence become the catalyst for greater division?

Only time will tell.

APPENDIX 1.5

> ## The Neko No Sanshimai
>
> 猫の三姉妹
>
> (The Three Cat Sisters)
>
> *Keepers of Balance*

Long ago, in the year 1232, Japan's provinces trembled beneath the firm grip of the Hojo Clan. The Hojo, with their unyielding commitment to loyalty and discipline, sought to extinguish any hint of rebellion before it could spark. Under their rule, chaos had no home, and order reigned supreme. But even as they controlled the hearts of men, whispers of greater threats reached their ears—whispers of beings who danced in the shadows of the natural world, capable of unmaking the fragile balance of existence.

In the following year, 1233, a lone adventurer by the name of Alberto Grace, arrived in Hojo lands, his voice heavy with tales of creatures neither human nor beast. Among these stories was the haunting spectre of vampires, beings whose very nature defied the laws of life and death. Though vampires had existed since the emergence of humans and other NetherKind, their rarity and reclusive nature rendered them more legend than reality. They were beings spoken of in hushed tones, their existence a thread of mystery that wove through the fabric of myth.

Fearing the chaos such beings could unleash, the Hojo gathered their wisest advisers and crafted a solution: an order that would protect not just the provinces but the natural world itself. Thus, the Neko No Sanshimai (猫の三姉妹)—the Three Cat Sisters—were born.

The first Sisters were not chosen by chance. They hailed from the Hojo Clan itself, distant relatives of the ruling family, said to carry a subtle connection to mysticism in their bloodline. This link to the unseen world was faint but enough to set them apart. Their selection ensured loyalty to the Hojo's vision while equipping the Sisters with the intuition and discipline needed for their sacred duty.

The Neko No Sanshimai's charge was clear: to preserve the balance of the natural world. While the Hojo focused their gaze on humans and demons alike, the Sisters walked a path between realms, watching for signs of unnatural disruption.

Their tools were many. Skilled fighters, they wielded weapons honed to perfection, each blow precise and deliberate. Yet, the Sisters were not without mysticism. It is said they could whisper to the winds, coaxing it to guide their blades or cloak their movements. They could light a path through darkness with a mere gesture or still the raging heart of a beast with a murmur. This mysticism was subtle, a quiet force that enhanced their skill without overshadowing it.

A Changing World

As decades passed, the Hojo's power faltered. By 1333, their reign crumbled, and with it, the Neko No Sanshimai's public presence. The Sisters slipped into the shadows, continuing their work unseen. From the forests to the mountains, their vigilance remained steadfast, though their names faded from memory.

Vampires, though rarely seen, remained a subject of fascination and fear. Their infrequent appearances were whispered about, and their power continued to inspire both awe and dread. For the Sisters, these whispers were enough to keep their guard up, ever wary of the balance tipping too far.

The Tragedy of 1406

One tale often whispered in darkened corners tells of a child born in 1406, a girl whose blood carried both human warmth and the icy chill of vampirism. To the Neko No Sanshimai, this child was no mere curiosity but a harbinger of calamity. Such a blending of worlds, they believed, could unravel the very fabric of nature.

Guided by their elder, the Sisters set out to find and end the child's existence. The task was grim, but their purpose left no room for hesitation. They silenced the girl and her parents, ensuring no trace of the family remained. Yet even as the mission was deemed complete, an unease settled over the Sisters. The air seemed heavier, the winds less sure. It was as though the act had left a mark not just on their souls but on the balance they sought to protect.

For years, they would speak of it in whispers—not regret, for they were resolute in their duty, but a lingering sense that something unnatural had been set loose. The world felt altered, and though no sign of immediate danger arose, the Sisters remained watchful, their resolve hardened.

The Present Day

Nestled in the vibrant streets of New Hinode, the Neko No Sanshimai have embraced a quieter existence while continuing their eternal watch. Their home and front for their activities is a quaint restaurant renowned for its artistry in creating delicacies that pay homage to the rich culinary traditions of Japan.

Inside, the ambience is serene, the soft hum of conversation blending with the gentle sounds of a trickling water feature.

While the meals they serve are exquisite—sushi crafted with precision, dishes that tell stories of their heritage—the restaurant is more than a culinary gem. It is a sanctuary, designed to soothe both body and spirit. Patrons are offered not just food but an experience meant to bring them a sense of balance. Sake flows freely alongside carefully prepared dishes, with the Sisters ensuring that every guest leaves feeling more centred than when they arrived. This quiet hospitality is a reflection of their mission: to restore harmony in all things.

In a small alcove, a Maneki-neko, or waving cat statue, sits with its perpetual motion. It is a talisman, attuned to the balance they vigilantly protect. As long as the world remains in harmony, the statue's cheerful arm sways. But when it falters, when the scales begin to tip, the statue becomes still. It is an unspoken signal that the Sisters must act. Meals are left unfinished, the serene atmosphere shifts, and the three women slip away into the city's labyrinthine alleys, their purpose clear and urgent.

Yet the elder mother of the Neko No Sanshimai carries a secret she has kept for years, one that binds her to her duty more tightly than her daughters can know.

Upon the birth of a child named Heidi, the cat's arm stopped waving. Though the balance was eventually restored, the elder knows that the event was no coincidence. Heidi's existence marks her as something unique—perhaps something dangerous. For now, the elder watches from afar, ensuring that Heidi lives her life unaware of her significance. The truth, she knows, will one day come to light.

The Legacy of the Sisters

The Neko No Sanshimai's impact extends far beyond New Hinode's streets. Though their restaurant remains a symbolic anchor, their mission often draws them to distant lands where the natural order is at risk. They have quelled raging storms brought on by supernatural forces, soothed the fury of spirits displaced from ancient shrines, and safeguarded the fragile ley lines that weave through the earth. Each action is undertaken with precision and secrecy, leaving no trace of their involvement save the restored balance.

Visitors to their restaurant often speak of an atmosphere unlike any other. It is not merely the food or the décor but something intangible—a sense of protection, of being watched over. They may notice the elder's eyes flicking toward the Maneki-neko or catch a fleeting moment where one of the Sisters pauses, her expression distant, as though sensing a shift beyond the room.

In rare moments, a guest might even find themselves drawn into the Sisters' quiet work. A passing word of insight or encouragement from one of them often lingers long after the meal is done, as if the Sisters' purpose extends beyond protecting the world—it is also about healing the people within it.

For those fortunate enough to visit, the experience is unforgettable. They leave not just with the memory of a perfect meal but with the quiet reassurance that someone, somewhere, ensures the world remains whole, no matter the cost.

APPENDIX 2: A Closer Look at the NetherKind Species

The NetherKind are not separate from humanity; they are part of the same world, interwoven into its societies, cultures, and progress. For as long as humans have built cities, sailed oceans, and forged civilizations, the NetherKind have stood alongside them—not as outsiders, but as equals, contributors, and, in some cases, the architects of history itself. They evolved alongside humanity, adapting to the same changing landscapes, conflicts, and advancements, their influence shaping everything from architecture and philosophy to medicine and innovation.

However, history has not always been kind to this shared existence. In the early 15th century, the Ash Dawn shattered the long-standing relationship between humans and

NetherKind. Driven by fear and misinformation, humanity turned against vampires, hunting them to the brink of extinction. The attack never extended to the other NetherKind species, but the message was clear—humans were capable of destruction on an unimaginable scale, and any species could be next. Faced with the undeniable reality of what had happened, the NetherKind withdrew, severing ties that had lasted for centuries.

In the wake of the Ash Dawn, the remaining NetherKind turned inward, building cities of their own—safe havens where they could thrive without fear of persecution. Though they adapted to life without humans at their side, the consequences of their separation lingered, shaping relationships, perceptions, and the way NetherKind navigate a world that was once shared without division. The Aetheren, already rare and elusive, faded even further into obscurity, their presence so infrequent that many question whether they still exist at all. Vampires, those who escaped the executions, vanished into hiding, rebuilding their dwindling numbers in small, isolated communities, cut off from the rest of the world.

This section offers a closer look at each species—not through their histories, but through what defines them. Their physiology, their instincts, their cultures, and the ways they have shaped and been shaped by the world around them. Some remain closely intertwined with humanity, while others exist on the edges, distant and unknown, but all continue to evolve in a world where the balance between past and present is still being rewritten.

APPENDIX 2.1

The Julpa Species

The Julpa are a deeply rooted NetherKind species, renowned for their physical strength, quiet wisdom, and profound connection to the natural world. They embody resilience and harmony with nature, preferring to live in tribal communities within vast forests, where they honour their ancestors and uphold traditions that have endured for centuries. Their history is filled with stories of protection, sacrifice, and unwavering unity, making them both formidable guardians and respected keepers of the past.

Physiology

The Julpa are towering, broad-shouldered figures with thick, leathery skin in earthy tones—stone greys, muted greens, and deep browns—that allow them to blend seamlessly into their forested environments. Their most distinctive features are their horns and multiple eyes, both of which define their identity and lineage.

A Julpa can have up to eight eyes, positioned across their broad faces. Their sharp vision allows them to perceive subtle movements, making them highly perceptive hunters and vigilant protectors.

Their horns, which grow in a variety of forms, are among their most defining features. Unlike other species where horn placement is consistent, Julpa horns emerge in different locations on each individual. Some extend like elephant tusks from the jaw, others grow like bison horns from the sides of the head, and some curve upwards from the forehead. The variety in structure is deeply symbolic, often linked to lineage, personal history, and spiritual significance.

Unlike simple growths, Julpa horns serve as living records of their experiences. Over time, they are carved with intricate patterns, marking significant life events, personal achievements, and moments of communal importance. Each set of horns tells a unique story, with older Julpa often regarded as living monuments of their tribe's history.

Unfortunately, the horns of fallen Julpa are highly sought after on the black market, treated as rare and valuable relics. Reports suggest they have surfaced in behind-closed-door auctions in Ch'i-Lin, a NetherKind city notorious for its questionable dealings and willingness to turn a blind eye if there's profit to be made. In the shadows of its trade markets, collectors and traffickers discreetly exchange these sacred remains, reducing what should be symbols of heritage and legacy to commodities for the highest bidder. Even more disturbingly, some Julpa have been targeted while alive, their horns and tusks forcibly removed and sold, a practice condemned by all NetherKind societies but difficult to fully eradicate.

Physically, the Julpa are immensely strong, their thick hides offering natural protection against harsh environments and even physical attacks. Their endurance makes them natural builders, hunters, and warriors, but their true strength lies in their unwavering sense of duty to their people.

Culture & Society

For centuries, the Julpa have lived in tightly knit tribal communities, their traditions woven into every aspect of their lives. They believe in the sanctity of the land, never taking more than they need and ensuring that the forests they inhabit remain untouched by greed. Their settlements, hidden deep within vast woodlands, are built using natural materials, blending seamlessly with their surroundings.

However, in the past century, many Julpa have chosen to leave their traditional ways behind, embracing the wider world and integrating into NetherKind cities where new opportunities await. While the younger generations seek out technology, trade, and new experiences, traditional ceremonies remain sacred, upheld by all Julpa—whether in the forests or the heart of a city.

One of their most sacred rites is The Rite of Marking, performed when a Julpa reaches adulthood. During this ceremony, a young Julpa receives their first carvings, etched by tribal elders to signify their readiness to begin their personal journey. Over time, the Julpa continue to carve their horns, turning them into living records of their lives.

Another key ritual is the Gathering of the Earth, a seasonal event where Julpa from various tribes and cities reunite to share stories, exchange resources, and reinforce the bonds that tie them together. The gathering features elaborate horn-carving displays, music, and communal feasts, celebrating unity and their connection to the land.

Ties to the World

The Julpa's influence extends beyond their forests, leaving a lasting mark on NetherKind history. One of the most enduring legends speaks of The Great Tusk, a mythical Julpa whose horns were said to have grown so vast they formed an archway over their settlement. The Great Tusk is celebrated as a unifying figure during one of the darkest times in NetherKind history, bringing together scattered groups to establish the first NetherKind city.

This legend has shaped the architectural symbolism of NetherKind cities. Every NetherKind city features an archway or monument honouring The Great Tusk, serving as a reminder of the Julpa's role as unifiers and protectors. These arches are iconic landmarks, embodying the ideals of strength and unity that transcend species.

Ties to Vampires and Humans

The Julpa share a unique and complex bond with vampires, forged during the Ash Dawn. When humanity sought to eradicate vampires, it was the Julpa who shielded them, offering protection in their forests and refusing to stand by as an entire species was wiped out. This act of solidarity saved countless lives and created a bond between the two species that persists to this day.

However, this act of compassion made the Julpa enemies of humanity. During the Ash Dawn, humans saw them as traitors for harbouring what they viewed as their greatest enemy. Even after the war ended, this bitterness lingered, creating lasting tensions between humans and the Julpa. Over the centuries, misunderstandings and prejudice have made peaceful coexistence rare, and in many parts of the world, Julpa are met with suspicion or hostility.

Even in NetherKind cities like Pazuzu, where integration is celebrated, humans often regard the Julpa with distrust, a reminder of old wounds that have never fully healed. Yet, despite this, the Julpa stand firm in their beliefs, refusing to let human resentment change the course of their traditions or values.

The Julpa in Modern Cities

While many Julpa remain in traditional tribal settings, others have chosen to build lives within NetherKind cities, where they are valued for their strength, craftsmanship, and unwavering sense of community. Their traditional carving skills are often employed in architectural design, sculpture, and monument creation, preserving NetherKind heritage in breathtaking works of art.

In cities, Julpa often gravitate toward roles that align with their values—guardianship, environmental stewardship, and construction. However, they remain deeply tied to their tribal roots, often returning home for ceremonies and spiritual reflection, ensuring that, no matter how far they roam, their traditions endure.

Why the Julpa Matter

The Julpa are a testament to strength, tradition, and resilience. Their carved horns tell stories of survival and heritage, while their actions—both past and present—speak to their unwavering commitment to protecting their people and their values. They are warriors when needed, builders when called upon, and guardians by nature, standing as a reminder that strength is not just physical—it is rooted in loyalty, community, and an unbreakable bond with the land they call home.

Despite the prejudices they face, the Julpa remain steadfast, a species that chooses integrity over fear, tradition over convenience, and loyalty over compromise. Whether deep in the forests or in the bustling streets of a NetherKind city, their presence is a reminder that some things are worth preserving—not just for themselves, but for the world they protect.

APPENDIX 2.2

The Nyssari Species

The Nyssari are a deeply attuned NetherKind species, known for their quiet presence and their ability to sense the shifting flow of the world around them. Unlike other NetherKind who exert control over their environments, the Nyssari exist in harmony with the spaces they inhabit, their strength rooted in observation and awareness rather than force. They are neither rulers nor warriors, yet their insight has shaped countless events throughout history, offering wisdom when others could only see chaos.

Physiology

The Nyssari are immediately recognizable by their varied shades of green skin, ranging from deep forest tones to muted moss and olive hues. This natural colouring allows them to blend effortlessly into their surroundings, whether in lush wilderness or shaded urban spaces. Their features are sharp and refined, carrying an elegant, ageless quality that makes them stand out even among other NetherKind.

Their eyes, often described as "windows to the unseen," have a reflective quality in dim light, allowing them to pick up even the subtlest of movements or changes in their environment. Though they lack the brute strength of species like the Julpa, their heightened awareness and agility enable them to navigate difficult terrain with remarkable precision.

While other NetherKind often shape the world around them, the Nyssari's physiology has adapted to perceive and respond to the world as it is. They are highly sensitive to atmospheric shifts—changes in air pressure, temperature, or even the presence of life around them—making them naturally attuned to subtle disturbances. While this ability has led to myths about their connection to the unseen, their awareness is deeply rooted in observation rather than mysticism.

Culture & Society

The Nyssari form small, tightly knit communities known as Circles, which serve as hubs of learning, reflection, and shared knowledge. Unlike hierarchical societies, Circles operate on mutual respect and understanding, with no single leader dictating their path. Decisions are made collectively, with each Nyssari contributing their insight before a course of action is chosen.

One of their most revered traditions is The Ritual of Flow, a practice used to attune themselves to the shifting patterns of their environment. Through quiet observation of moving elements—drifting water, swaying leaves, or shifting sands—they seek clarity in moments of uncertainty. While some dismiss these practices as superstition, many Nyssari believe that aligning with the natural flow of events allows them to anticipate change rather than be caught off guard by it.

Despite their preference for peace, they are not passive. When necessary, they intervene in subtle yet effective ways—redirecting conflict, influencing outcomes without force, and ensuring balance is maintained. Their reluctance to engage in direct confrontation has led some to view them as overly cautious, but those who have witnessed their methods firsthand recognize that power does not always come from action.

Ties to the World

The Nyssari have existed alongside other species for centuries, yet their presence has often gone unnoticed. While they do not seek power, they have played a quiet role in shaping NetherKind history. Their ability to sense and interpret change has made them invaluable as advisers, negotiators, and observers, though their involvement is rarely recorded in the annals of history.

One enduring legend speaks of The Silent Path, an ancient trail known only to the Nyssari. It is said that those who walk it with purpose will be led to where they are most needed, whether that be a place of refuge, revelation, or confrontation. Some claim that the path is ever-changing, a test for those who seek it, while others believe it to be a metaphor for the Nyssari's way of navigating the world—always moving, always adapting.

Ties to Vampires and Humans

The Nyssari share an unspoken understanding with vampires, a connection forged in the quiet spaces between survival and secrecy. During the Ash Dawn, it was the Nyssari who guided fleeing vampires to hidden refuges, using their knowledge of the world's unseen currents to keep them safe. While the two species rarely interact in structured societies, there exists a mutual respect between them—a silent acknowledgment of shared isolation.

With humans, their relationship is more complex. While they hold no historical grudges, they have watched human civilizations expand recklessly, often at the cost of the natural world. Their efforts to encourage coexistence have largely been ignored, leading many Nyssari to withdraw from direct involvement with human affairs. However, some have taken a different approach, choosing to work within human society to influence change rather than resist it from the outside.

The Nyssari in Modern NetherKind Cities

Though often perceived as reclusive, the Nyssari are far from absent in modern NetherKind society. While some continue to live in more isolated Circles, others have established a presence within NetherKind cities, where their insights are valued in matters of diplomacy, strategy, and societal development.

In Pazuzu City, a small group of Nyssari maintain a sanctuary at the city's edge, where flowing water and lush gardens provide a space for reflection and quiet counsel. Unlike other institutions, this sanctuary is not a temple or a place of worship—it is simply a haven where those seeking clarity can come without judgment. Outsiders often find their presence both grounding and unsettling, a paradox that reflects the Nyssari's ability to sense what others ignore. While they rarely intervene in city affairs, their wisdom has been sought during pivotal moments of unrest, their guidance valued even by those who doubt their methods.

Why the Nyssari Matter

The Nyssari's legacy is not one of dominance or force, but of awareness. They are a reminder that power does not always lie in strength and that wisdom does not always require words. While others seek to shape the world through action, the Nyssari shape it through understanding, existing as quiet custodians of balance in a world that often overlooks it.

They do not demand recognition, nor do they seek control. They exist as part of the world, neither above it nor outside it, ensuring that even in the midst of change, the delicate equilibrium of existence is never truly forgotten.

APPENDIX 2.3

The Vaylen Species

The Vaylen are a NetherKind species defined by their mastery of craftsmanship, trade, and precision. They are creators, innovators, and problem solvers, blending artistry with purpose in everything they do. Unlike species driven by mysticism or brute force, the Vaylen thrive in structured collaboration, where everything they build—whether physical or conceptual—serves a purpose. Their influence is found in the grand structures of NetherKind cities, the hidden pathways beneath them, and the intricate details woven into the tools, machines, and artistry that support their world.

Physiology

The Vaylen are the most adaptable of all NetherKind species, a trait reflected in their versatile physiology. Their builds vary more than other species, allowing them to excel in different environments and professions. Some are more compact and muscular, suited to hands-on construction or mechanical work, while others are leaner and more agile, favoring precision-based disciplines like engineering and medicine. Their skin, ranging in muted metallic undertones, holds a subtle sheen that hints at their species' unique resilience without appearing unnatural.

A defining trait of the Vaylen is their bioluminescent markings, intricate geometric patterns that emerge across their skin in dim light. These designs, unique to each individual, shift in response to their emotional state and focus, forming a visual language that allows them to communicate unspoken thoughts and intentions. While they view this as an extension of their identity, many outsiders—particularly humans—find these shifting patterns unreadable, adding to the perception of the Vaylen as distant or secretive.

Their hands are adapted for precision, with slightly elongated fingers and naturally reinforced nails that allow for intricate craftsmanship. Many Vaylen wear functional adornments such as segmented rings, layered cuffs, or tool-integrated gloves, each piece often custom-crafted to serve both aesthetic and practical purposes.

Culture & Society

Vaylen society operates within a guild system, where individuals dedicate themselves to disciplines such as engineering, medicine, architecture, or trade. Unlike rigid hierarchical structures, Vaylen Guilds encourage flexibility, allowing members to shift between professions over time, refining their expertise while contributing to various fields.

One of the most valued principles among the Vaylen is "Structure Without Waste," a belief that everything must serve a function, whether physical, intellectual, or philosophical. To them, there is no beauty in excess, no virtue in meaningless traditions. The pursuit of mastery is not just about knowledge—it is about applying knowledge in ways that enhance the world around them.

While other NetherKind species may define themselves through history or ritual, the Vaylen define themselves by what they build and what they leave behind. Whether through reinforced city walls, medical advancements, or intricately crafted mechanisms, their contributions are enduring, tangible, and essential to the continued survival of NetherKind civilization.

Ties to the World

Throughout NetherKind history, the Vaylen have been instrumental in shaping the physical foundations of society. While they are not warriors, their fortifications have withstood sieges, and while they are not rulers, their designs have dictated the layouts of cities and infrastructure.

During The Siege of 1507, when Pazuzu City was besieged by human forces, the Vaylen played a crucial role in engineering defenses that allowed the city to hold out. Their network of hidden tunnels and reinforced structures ensured that vital supplies could be moved unseen, and their quick-thinking innovations turned the tide of battle more than once. Even today, the Veiled Paths, a labyrinth beneath Pazuzu, remain one of the most significant testaments to their ingenuity, with many of its original structures still in use.

Their bioluminescent patterns were also invaluable during such crises. In complete darkness, they became natural waypoints for their allies, guiding NetherKind through hidden corridors or signaling warnings in silence. The practicality of their abilities has long been acknowledged, earning them a reputation as problem solvers who find solutions where others see obstacles.

Ties to Other Species

Humans and the Vaylen have shared a long history of trade, innovation, and knowledge exchange. While the Vaylen's reserved nature sometimes leads to mistrust, they have never been seen as adversaries. Instead, humans have often sought them out as craftsmen, scholars, and engineers. However, the Vaylen approach their dealings with humans carefully, ensuring that any advancements shared do not pose a risk to the balance of power within NetherKind society.

Julpa and the Vaylen share a mutual respect, particularly in craftsmanship. While the Julpa excel in raw carving and physical construction, the Vaylen refine and design intricate details, leading to collaborative works that blend strength with precision. In Sachamama, it is not uncommon to see Julpa stonework infused with Vaylen precision-carved metal inlays, showcasing the fusion of their talents.

The Nyssari and the Vaylen hold philosophical differences but occasionally align in matters of long-term planning and maintaining order. The Nyssari believe that balance arises naturally if left undisturbed, choosing to observe and adapt rather than impose control. The Vaylen, by contrast, see balance as something that must be actively designed and maintained, creating systems and structures to ensure stability where none might naturally exist.

The Vaylen in Modern NetherKind Cities

The Vaylen are deeply integrated into NetherKind cities, where their expertise is invaluable in maintaining infrastructure, technological advancements, and urban planning. In Pazuzu, they oversee the maintenance of key structures, including bridges, aqueducts, and subterranean pathways. In Kimaris, they help balance the city's delicate relationship with its lake surroundings, designing sustainable solutions to ensure its longevity.

Unlike more reclusive species, the Vaylen embrace modernization and progress, blending tradition with advancement in ways that benefit all NetherKind. Their influence extends beyond physical structures; they are sought-after in fields such as medicine, engineering, and mechanics, where their ability to analyze and refine processes makes them pioneers in their fields.

Despite this, they remain somewhat enigmatic to outsiders. Their reserved nature and precise way of thinking can make them appear detached or calculating, leading some to mistake their pragmatism for indifference. However, those who understand the Vaylen know that everything they do is driven by a desire to refine, improve, and create a world where balance is achieved through innovation rather than destruction.

Why the Vaylen Matter

The Vaylen do not shape the world through conquest or mysticism—they shape it through their hands, their ideas, and their ability to build lasting foundations. Their bioluminescent patterns, once merely a biological quirk, have become guiding lights in times of crisis. Their structures, innovations, and inventions stand as testaments to their pursuit of balance and precision.

In a world where chaos and instability often threaten the delicate order of NetherKind society, the Vaylen offer structure, reason, and ingenuity. They are not rulers, nor do they seek dominance—but without them, the cities, fortresses, and very foundations of the NetherKind world would crumble. Their legacy is one of creation, refinement, and an unwavering dedication to ensuring that progress is never left to chance, but instead shaped with intention and purpose.

APPENDIX 2.4

The Vampire Species

Vampires remain one of the most enigmatic and scarce NetherKind species, their presence more often felt in whispered tales than in everyday life. Unlike other NetherKind, they have no means of natural reproduction, making their survival a rare and deliberate choice rather than an inevitability. Their existence is shrouded in discipline, resilience, and secrecy, and while other species have integrated into broader NetherKind and human societies, vampires remain largely nomadic, their numbers few, their communities hidden.

Physiology

Vampires have an unnerving stillness to them, their movements precise and deliberate, never wasted. Their skin is pale, sometimes appearing almost colourless in certain lighting, and their eyes always carry a red hue, which becomes more pronounced in dim environments. Though they share the same physical form as humans, there is a sharpness to their features, an intensity in the way they carry themselves that sets them apart.

Perhaps their most well-known trait is their vulnerability to sunlight. Exposure to direct sunlight results in a rapid and irreversible burning process, reducing them to ash in mere moments. This forces them to seek shelter in locations where natural barriers provide protection or construct hidden sanctuaries deep underground.

Another notable characteristic is their greatly reduced aging process. While it is evident that vampires age far more slowly than humans, the limits of their lifespan remain unknown. Some appear unchanged for centuries, while others eventually show signs of age—though at a vastly different pace from any human. This has led to speculation among scholars and the NetherKind alike as to whether vampires eventually die of old age or if other factors determine their longevity.

While vampires rarely display their full physical capabilities, their strength and ferocity have been recorded in moments of true desperation. Their existence is mostly hidden, controlled, and secretive, making direct encounters with their raw power exceedingly rare. However, historical accounts—particularly from the Ash Dawn—paint a far grimmer picture. Facing extermination, vampires were seen tearing through their attackers with overwhelming force, their speed and precision turning battles into massacres. These rare moments of unleashed power only heightened the fear humans held toward them, reinforcing the belief that vampires were an existential threat that needed to be eradicated.

Culture & Society

Vampires do not reproduce naturally, which has shaped their culture into one of careful selection and strict traditions. Outsiders who wish to join their ranks must first integrate into vampire society, living among them for extended periods to fully immerse themselves in their customs. Only then, after long deliberation, will the vampires extend an invitation for transformation—a ceremonial process that involves an exchange of blood and a period of rest in absolute darkness. This process is never forced, and only those who align with their way of life are chosen.

Despite their isolation, vampires have a rich oral tradition, with history preserved through stories, symbols, and carved Memoriam Stones—engraved markers left in hidden settlements to honour their fallen and record their history. Each stone tells a story, encoded through intricate patterns, ensuring that even if their kind is lost, their past will not be forgotten.

Ties to the World

Vampires are unique among the NetherKind in that they did not evolve naturally. Their origins remain a mystery, and while legends differ, many speak of a singular progenitor—Silas. Whether an alchemical accident or a divine punishment, Silas is said to have been the first vampire, wandering alone until encountering others who shared their fate. Some believe Silas still exists somewhere in the world, their legacy surviving through the stories passed down by their kind.

Speculation persists that the first vampire was once human. This theory, fuelled by the fact that only humans can survive the transformation, has led to debates among scholars and conspiracy theorists alike. Some believe Silas was the result of an ancient experiment gone wrong; others suggest something more deliberate. Regardless of the truth, this unique link to humanity heightened the fear that led to the Ash Dawn.

During the height of vampire persecution, humans saw themselves as livestock, believing that, given enough time, all of humanity would either be turned or devoured. The hysteria that followed fuelled an unprecedented extermination campaign, forcing the remaining vampires into hiding. While no other NetherKind species were directly targeted, the Ash Dawn served as a chilling reminder of what humans were capable of, causing many species to withdraw from human society altogether.

Despite the centuries of separation, some NetherKind species stepped forward to aid vampires in their time of need. The Julpa provided shelter deep within their forests, while the Nyssari guided fleeing vampires to hidden sanctuaries. This act of solidarity forged lasting bonds between vampires and the other NetherKind—though with an ironic twist. Vampires, despite their deep mistrust of humans, remain entirely reliant on them to sustain their species. The very beings they fear and avoid are the only ones capable of increasing their numbers, a fact that continues to shape their fragile place in the world.

While most vampires remain hidden, some have found a rare sanctuary in places where darkness is prolonged. One such settlement, The Eternal Haven, exists in Svalbard, Norway, where polar nights stretch for months. Here, vampires have built a thriving community, free from the constant threat of sunlight, proving that even in the most inhospitable places, their kind can endure.

Why Vampires Matter

Vampires are a contradiction—fragile yet enduring, feared yet misunderstood. Their history is a testament to survival against impossible odds, a reminder of what it means to adapt when the world seeks to erase you. As one of the most persecuted NetherKind species, they have endured through secrecy and resilience, their presence lingering in the spaces between legend and reality. Though their numbers are few, they are the silent observers of a world that has long sought to forget them.

APPENDIX 2.5

The Aetherien Species

The Aetherien are a NetherKind species shrouded in mystery, known as the silent guides of the departed. More than mere watchers of death, they exist at the thresholds of great change, drawn to moments where life and the unknown converge. Whether it is the passing of a soul, the eruption of tragedy, or the dawn of something new, their presence signals that the Veil—the boundary between existence and oblivion—is shifting.

Their role is neither to summon nor to control but to ensure that what is lost finds its way, preventing the disruption of the natural order. Unlike other NetherKind, they do not engage in politics or seek influence, yet their rare appearances invoke both awe and unease. To some, they are guides. To others, omens of an inevitable fate.

The Aetherien appear at times when the world is on the verge of a major shift. This turning point could lead to disaster or a moment of great significance, but even the Aetherien themselves do not always know why they are drawn to a place until the event unfolds.

Physiology

Aetherien appear humanoid but carry an unsettling, ethereal presence. Their translucent skin glows faintly in darkness, revealing intricate patterns that ripple like water currents. These markings shift subtly in response to nearby disturbances in the balance of life and death, making it seem as if the Aetherien themselves are reflections of unseen forces.

Their eyes are deep pools of silvery-grey or shadowed black, appearing as if they absorb light rather than reflect it. Many describe the sensation of being gazed upon by an

Aetherien as an unnerving experience, as if their very essence is being seen in its entirety.

Their movements are fluid yet deliberate, carrying an eerie grace as though they are moving in time with something just beyond perception. When they pass, the air around them feels heavier, and the world itself seems to pause for a moment.

Culture and Society

The Aetherien have no known cities, no recorded settlements, and no structured civilisation as other NetherKind do. They exist in scattered enclaves, moving where they are needed rather than rooting themselves in any one place. Some believe they dwell within the Veil itself, stepping between existence and the unknown, though this has never been proven.

Their purpose is to ensure the proper passage of life into death, guiding the lost towards rest and preventing the unnatural tethering of souls to the world of the living. They are not necromancers nor spirit-talkers, but rather guardians against imbalance, ensuring that nothing lingers where it does not belong.

Though they do not live in conventional societies, Aetherien are known to gather in silent, ceremonial observances when significant events threaten to disrupt the natural order. These gatherings, known as Binding Songs, are performed in times of immense tragedy, often at sites where death and suffering have left a deep scar on the world. Witnesses describe these rituals as hauntingly beautiful yet incomprehensible, with no clear explanation of their purpose beyond the restoration of balance.

Ties to the World

Aetherien are not rulers, builders, or warriors, yet their presence has shaped NetherKind history in ways few understand. They do not seek out conflict, but they do not ignore it either. In times of great loss, they have been seen guiding both humans and NetherKind towards peace, ensuring that devastation does not leave wounds upon the world too deep to heal.

One of the most well-known events involving the Aetherien is The Mourning Circle, which took place during the Ash Dawn. As vampires were hunted to the brink of extinction, a group of Aetherien gathered in a desolate wasteland, guiding countless lost souls to their rest. It is said that without them, the weight of such mass death might have permanently fractured the Veil, unleashing chaos upon the world. The site of the Mourning Circle remains undisturbed, and no Aetherien have returned to it since.

Another legend tells of The Day of the Still Wind, when an Aetherien appeared in a quiet village hours before it was consumed by a sudden flood. Witnesses recall the air becoming unnaturally heavy and the Aetherien walking the streets in silence, glancing at the townsfolk as if preparing them for what was to come. When the floodwaters arrived, those who survived described an eerie sense of calm in their final moments, as if they had already accepted their fate.

Ties to Other Species

Vampires and Aetherien share an unspoken connection. Vampires, existing on the precipice between life and death, hold an almost magnetic pull for the Aetherien, who appear momentarily transfixed in their presence. The reason for this is unknown, though some speculate that Aetherien perceive vampires as anomalies—beings who should have crossed into death but never did. Strangely, vampires often find comfort in the presence of Aetherien, as if instinctively recognising a kindred spirit.

Humans regard Aetherien with unease, as their presence is often associated with great loss. To some, they are angels of mercy, guiding souls to peace. To others, they are harbingers of doom, arriving only when tragedy is imminent.

Their neutral stance in mortal affairs means they are neither friend nor foe, but their reputation ensures that most people, when faced with an Aetherien, whisper prayers in fear.

Nyssari and Aetherien share an appreciation for patience and observation, though the Nyssari tend to focus on the tangible world, while the Aetherien move between what is seen and unseen. The two species rarely interact, but when they do, it is often in moments of reflection rather than conversation.

Julpa and Aetherien have little reason to cross paths, though Julpa oral histories mention encounters where Aetherien appeared before great migrations or wars, silently acknowledging the turning points in their species' history. Some Julpa shamans consider an Aetherien's arrival a sign to either move forward or prepare for hardship.

Vaylen and Aetherien exist at opposite ends of understanding. The Vaylen believe in shaping their environment to create stability, while the Aetherien see their purpose as maintaining balance by ensuring the natural order is not disrupted. While they do not oppose each other, their philosophies rarely align, meaning encounters between the two are brief and often filled with mutual curiosity.

The Aetherien in Modern NetherKind Cities

Aetherien rarely remain in any city for long. When they do, they are silent observers, never interfering unless the balance of life and death is at risk. Some NetherKind cities, such as Malphas and Arunasura, have learned to recognise their presence as a sign of great change approaching—whether that change is good or ill remains unknown.

Despite their rarity, Aetherien myths permeate NetherKind culture, and their influence is felt even when they are absent. Many NetherKind still leave offerings at crossroads or upon graves in hopes of gaining an Aetherien's silent blessing, ensuring a peaceful passage into the afterlife.

Why the Aetherien Matter

The Aetherien stand as the quiet sentinels of life and death, their existence a reminder of the unseen forces that shape the world. Their ability to guide, sense, and act at moments of great transition ensures the balance of the Veil remains intact. Their rare connection with vampires underscores their role as observers of liminal spaces, embodying the fragility and inevitability of change.

Through their quiet vigilance and profound purpose, they remain one of the most enigmatic and essential NetherKind species.

Printed in Great Britain
by Amazon